Chasm of Talent

Chasm of Talent

For my Dad

Prologue

Icilius Kelelm, newly ordained Paladin of the Unbroken Church, stared down at the small leather bound chest in his hands. The chest was old, simply made and no larger than a loaf of bread. Within rested something that would unlock his true potential, making him a tool for the Eternal that would cause unbelievers and blasphemers to quake in fear.

The chest and its contents belonged to his father, Fen, as it had belonged his grandfather and great grandfather previously, before Fen had given up his life in service to the Church. The very room Icilius currently resided in, sparse, square and identical to the hundreds of others that occupied the Cleric's dormitory, was where the past two generations of Kelelms had risen to greatness, in service to the Eternal. Icilius undid the clasp and opened the lid to reveal a thick silver bracelet, adorned with a single clear gemstone the size of a golden mir coin of the Realm.

Icilius had spent three of his twenty years working toward this moment, training his body and his mind. He could not stop his fingers from trembling slightly as they touched the bracelet, still faintly warm as if it had been worn just moments before.

He held the bracelet in his hand a moment, marveling at how light it was for its size and slid the bracelet on his right wrist. Icilius took a deep breath and closed the bracelet around his wrist, the clasp so cunningly wrought, no seam showed once it was closed. He grimaced slightly as two thick needles stabbed into his wrist from just beneath the clear gemstone. The pain did not lessen as the needles remained embedded in his flesh, but he scarcely noticed as he concentrated on the stone.

A small dot of color appeared in the depths of the stone. In the dim light of his room, it appeared almost black though it wasn't. Icilius watched with bated breath as the stone filled with his blood, now resembling a polished ruby of the finest quality. He felt a low rush of tingles spread across his body as the fatigue accrued from staying up all night in prayer disappeared. Icilius knew the increased vitality would happen but experiencing it was something else entirely, as was the new sensation of a vast reservoir of potential power emanating from the Blessing, tempting as sin.

He held up his right hand in front of his eyes and made a fist, pleased the embedded needles did not pull at his flesh. The two needles would remain in his skin for the rest of his life, the entire bracelet now a part of him as much as his fingers. While wearing the bracelet, he would be able to run fast enough to pass a horse at full gallop, lift several times his own weight, see something a mile off as clearly as if it were a pace away, or a dozen other feats. His blood let him do these things, though admittedly not for very long, and each feat drained some of the blood from the stone. When the stone was once more clear, it would slowly refill again.

Wearing the bracelet would, of course, shorten the years of his life considerably; Icilius had never heard of a Paladin of the Church living much past their fortieth name day, but, considering the aid he could lend to the Church and how he could enforce the edicts of the Eternal across a broken and morally corrupt land, it was a small and just price to pay.

A single knock at his door brought his head around, and Icilius realized he had been standing stock still, staring at the Eternal's Blessing on his wrist. Icilius opened the door of his room to find Markus, a Paladin a few years his senior, standing in the hall, admiring one of his thick gold rings.

Markus was one of the few Paladins who held two Blessings and, while the stones on each ring were smaller than Icilius's, using them both in tandem made him one of the most powerful Paladins in all of Irillia, not far behind the Regent himself. Markus tended to have an inflated opinion of himself because of this, not a trait he should possess as a Paladin. Still, he was a friend, so Icilius never voiced his opinion aloud.

"Come along, Icilius. You don't want to be late for your first Conclave." Markus's eyes fell on Icilius's Blessing, and considered it for a moment without comment, as remarking on other's Blessings was considered rude, in the same way one did not comment on a woman's weight. "Shall we race there so you can put your Blessing to the test?"

"No, I don't think so," Icilius said, and although frivolous use of the Blessing was tantamount to blasphemy, he did consider it for a moment. For the briefest of moments.

Their travel through the Citadel was short, and even though Icilius had lived there for nearly five years, he felt a sense of ownership he never had before, having the Blessing firmly on his wrist. He could remember a time when he'd scrubbed the very stones beneath his feet, in penance for some minor, self-reported infraction, though the memory seemed a lifetime and more in the past. He swelled with pride as he looked over the rich tapestries and ornate carvings filling every niche in the walls, and smiled warmly at the sight of the young Novices as they rushed about on errands.

When the two Paladins reached the meeting hall, a wide, airy chamber with high stained-glass windows, they found it nearly full, mostly with Clerics, the newest initiates into the Church. The Clerics were ordained to go out into the land and spread the word of the Eternal and all the good that could be accomplished by following His teachings. Icilius and Markus moved along the rows of backless benches to the single row of hard backed chairs at the front of the room reserved for Paladins.

There were only eight in attendance; the others were out across Irillia, taking part in *Operation Decimation*, a top secret tactical maneuver, the details of which Icilius had not been privy to as a Cleric. All together, there were fewer than three dozen Paladins in all of Irillia, and Icilius felt a thrill race through him as he took his seat among those gathered. Only a few moments after he sat, the High Regent himself came in through a side door and walked over to the circular dais at the front of the room. As soon as his highly polished shoe touched the dais, all conversation in the room stopped as if cut off by an ax. The High Regent was an older man with bushy eyebrows over eyes the hue and firmness of frozen iron, walking with perfect posture as his gold-edged white robes shone brilliantly. He raised his hands over the seated gathering and every head in the room bowed as one. He blessed them with a strong voice, using the *Vorlathian* tongue, which had not been spoken by any, save members of the Unbroken Church in over two centuries. It was a formal prayer, longer than Icilius expected for the start of a Conclave.

He ended the prayer with the usual benediction and everyone in the room looked up. "My sons, I have called you here to announce this year, we will once again have our Great Pilgrimage." He paused, as if expecting some loud reaction from his audience, though one was not forthcoming. Icilius could hear excited shifting in the seats behind him and could almost feel everyone in the room leaning forward expectantly.

The High Regent allowed himself a small, fatherly smile before continuing. "In just a few day's time, Regent Loric will lead all remaining Paladins and a support staff of one hundred Clerics out into Irillia, heading north, to spread the Word of the Eternal into every hamlet, village and city, while seeking out any blasphemers who may have escaped local governmental justice and meting out punishment as directed by the Eternal's commands." He paused once more, and his piercingly clear eyes swept the room like a ray of reflected sunlight.

Icilius grinned inwardly during the pause; he, along with every other person present, knew 'blasphemers' meant the Eternal accursed Azoreans, blighted men and woman stricken with gray scaly patches on their skin, scourged hearts which had no place amongst the rest of Irillia's Eternal-fearing populace.

"In addition to spreading the Word of the Eternal, you will also amass an army of fighting men with the goal of laying siege to the bowels of the Middle Realm, home to a teeming nest of Azorean scum, kill all those who resist and bring the rest back to our Citadel for trial under the Eternal's grace!"

At these words, every man present rose as one and loudly applauded. Icilius kept an ear open for any unseemly shouts or other excited exultation, but everyone respected the sanctity of the Conclave. The High Regent smiled and allowed the applause to go on for several moments before he made a slight gesture with his hand. The applause then ceased, and everyone took their seats.

"A culling on this scale has never before been attempted, but I am certain the Eternal will smile upon you, and success will be yours. After cleaning out the dregs of the Middle Realm, you will continue into the Northern Realm where the Word of the Eternal is not . . ." The High Regent's words rolled over Icilius, who tried to put his full attention to listening; he could not stop himself from excitedly picturing his first encounter with the accursed Azoreans, bringing them to the justice of the Unbroken Church. He sent up a silent prayer of thanks to the Eternal for the opportunity to do his good works. Icilius couldn't wait to get started.

Chapter One

Owin Cadmon, unaware his life would irrevocably change in a few short hours, stood at the base of the tallest Altus tree in all of Vridian Ford and looked up at the lowest branches, nearly twenty feet straight up. His father, the mayor of their village, once told him climbing a tree was like ascending a ladder, though Owin suspected his father had never put his claim into practice, certainly not with this tree.

Owin liked to take the path of least resistance, which normally excluded physical labor like tree climbing. However, with both his mother and older sister out looking for him, bodily exertion would be that path.

He glanced about to see if anyone was watching; he was on the far side of the tree from the village green in the center of Vridian Ford, but it never hurt to be careful. All it would take would be for one gossiping villager to take note of him, and all his careful skulking would be for naught.

Green and yellow vines tightly encircled the wide trunk of the tree, spiraling upward. These vines normally grew thick, spade-shaped leaves, but these all had been pulled off in a wide swath leading straight up the side of the tree.

Owin reached up and took hold of one of the vines and began to climb, easily finding toeholds and handholds wedged in between the vines by previous climbers. He soon passed the lowest boughs and kept climbing. His destination was the broad wooden platform encircling the trunk of the tree and supported by wooden slats, still a dozen feet or so overhead. It was one of several old guard platforms which at one time ringed the village on all sides; this was the only one remaining.

Owin paused a moment and wiped sweat off his forehead with the sleeve of his shirt and reflected perhaps climbing was more trouble than it was worth; however, sometimes he felt as if he just had to get away to be by himself for a time. Two sisters did not make a large family, not compared to those living on the farms off to the south of Vridian Ford, but somehow when you were the firstborn son of the mayor, you were expected to behave a certain way which was just exhausting. What good was it having a mayor for a father if every other villager seemed to be watching his every move and drawing up a tally of misdeeds to report to his parents?

He chose to continue his climb and, a few moments later, pulled himself through the gap near the trunk and simply lay on the surface of the platform, his cheek against the cool, slightly moist wood, while he caught his breath. He listened to the nearest branches shift slightly in the wind and breathed in the deep, wet smell of the tree; he frowned to himself as he caught a whiff of old sweat and the sharp sting of hard liquor, which had no business being there.

Owin climbed to his feet, wondering if someone had thrown a little party there on the old guard tower without inviting him. He circled the wide platform around the tree until he came back to where he began and saw no sign of anyone else having been there, save for a small pile of what looked like empty grain sacks piled against the trunk.

Owin left them where they lay and turned to stand at the platform's waist high railing, worn smooth as a polished river stone from time and countless grasping hands. He rested his elbows on the railing and watched the townsfolk of Vridian Ford go about their business, perhaps a dozen or so yards below.

He watched for nearly a half an hour in silence, smiling slightly to himself as he caught sight of his older sister skirting the far side of the village green, her swift stride bespeaking nothing but determined purpose, even from that distance. That single-mindedness might one day allow her to become the first Mayoress of their village, according to many residents, including herself.

A sound very like a rusted saw with bent teeth passing against the grain of a log of hardwood pulled his gaze from his sister, and he looked directly down the length of the trunk, leaning slightly over the rail. As ridiculous as it seemed, Owin thought someone was trying to saw through the massive trunk of the tree, though he saw no one near on the ground, and then the same rasping sound came again, this time sounding much closer.

Owin looked again at the pile of empty grain sacks and saw the pile rise slightly in the middle, creating a defined hill. He looked more closely and saw the unmistakable heel of a boot poking out from underneath one of the sacks, so he kicked it with the toe of his own boot.

The boot's owner jerked awake in mid-snore, sitting bolt upright and causing the pile of burlap sacks to slide off and puddle around him, revealing an old man, mostly bald save for a thick ring of gray hair encircling his head like a halo. A small clay jug lay on its side next to the man, who turned his attention to it before staring blearily up at Owin. "By the never-ending beard of the Eternal, Owin, can't a man have half a mo' of rest?"

Owin glanced up at the mid morning sun slating through the boughs. "How much more do you need, Jem? What are you doing up here?"

"I'm sleeping it off, of course. D'you think I was picking flowers?" Jem dug knobby knuckles into his eyes and blinked several times.

"Jem, even children not yet off apron strings know that. Why here? You're lucky not to have fallen off."

"I'm as nimble as a squirrel when it comes to trees." He thrust a gnarled hand into the air. "Help an old man up?" Owin grasped his hand and pulled him to his feet, catching a whiff of onion and hard liquor for his troubles. Jem wore a baggy, stained gray shirt unlaced at his throat and voluminous black trousers jammed into his boots.

"Is this your secret place to sleep a few off?" Owin asked.

Jem waved a finger in front of his face as if to tap the side of his nose but missed. "One of several. Wouldn't do to present myself at home in me cups. My dear wife would've broken another broom handle over my head."

Jem moved over to stand at the railing and took a deep breath of air, drawing in more than Owin would have thought could fit in his thin chest. "Ah. Yet another day in Vridian Ford. Just another unimportant village in the Northern Realm. D'you know I live in this village because the taxes are so low?"

Owin nodded, though Jem didn't seem to be expecting a response. Owin knew it was the worst kept secret in the village Jem was very well off, despite his shabby clothes and preference of the cheapest spirits.

"Taxes, my young friend, taxes. If ever there was proof of how far Irillia has fallen from what the Eternal planned for us, it's taxes." Jem leaned against the wide tree trunk, a curved white pipe in his hand, the bowl intricately carved. He gestured with the unlit pipe grandly as he spoke, emphasizing his points with the stem. "Taxes, of course, are the lifeblood of the government, especially for our dear House of Commons . . ."

Letting the old man's words wash over him like a light rain, Owin propped his elbows on the railing and stared down at the village green. He listened with less than half an ear to Jem's complaining about how the House was filled with argumentative fools who never got anything done without a month's worth of speeches and squabbling, nodding occasionally to give the impression he was listening.

Owin watched old Cilla Brown, the headmistress of Vridian Ford's only schoolroom, stride purposefully across the green, passing Hobb Kepple and giving a curt nod to his raising of his hat. Even though Owin had finished school over a year ago, Cilla was someone he went out of his way to avoid, as it seemed her favorite pastime was telling tales. He watched the local leathersmith Elver Dunmire make a beeline across the far edge of the green, his arms filled with what looked like bolts of cloth.

He continued watching until he realized Jem had finished berating both the House of Commons and the King of the Southern Realm and had moved on to describe why the Os'Nurians, a small force of men and women who could bend and shape primitive elements of the world to their will, should never have been allowed to gather together nor given special deputization by the rulers of both Realms to meddle in all affairs.

Owin had heard this particular lecture before and decided his mother and sister ought to have given up looking for him by now, so it should be safe for him to have a late morning nap before the midday meal. He interrupted Jem in mid-sentence. "Well, I'm off for a nap, Jem. Nice talking to you."

Jem, who was used to more forceful interruptions, sometimes accompanied by an empty mug thrown in his general direction, blinked in surprise. "Quite a good idea, Owin." He glanced up at the position of the sunlight filtering through the boughs. "I could do for a lie down meself, 'specially since old Thad refuses to serve me before midday."

Owin smiled to himself as he climbed down. His last sight of Jem was the old man lying back down on the pile of canvas sacks, using the empty jug for a pillow.

Owin reached his bedroom without trouble; one of the few benefits of having a mayor for a father was his mother, as a mayor's wife, was often as busy as her husband, running Vridian Ford Women's Council, among a dozen other things. Owin found his room just as he left it: bed unmade, curtain drawn over the small square glass window over his bedstead.

He sat on the edge of the mattress, tugged off his boots then lay down and closed his eyes. He was nearly asleep when he heard a slight flutter over his head, like wings on the wind. A moment later, he heard the same noise again and thought it must have been the curtain blowing over his head. The third time, he distinctly felt something glide past his face, brushing lightly against his nose.

Owin sat up and looked about his darkened room, finding it empty. He glanced at the half-open bedroom door but could not perceive any movement in the hall beyond. He began to lay back down when he heard the sound of paper crinkling beneath him. Owin reached back and pulled out a folded paper dart, now slightly crumpled. He looked over the rumpled bed clothes and saw two other paper darts lying on the bed.

Owin smiled, crumpled up the dart in his hand into a ball and threw it out into the hallway. It struck the floor and rolled out of sight, eliciting a gasp from behind the bedroom door. "Seri, if you come in here, I'll show you how to make a better dart."

Owin's sister, barely six years old and filled with twice as much mischief as he remembered having, popped into view in the hall and flew into his room, a long braid flying behind her like a banner. She leapt into his bed, and Owin tickled her under the arms. She tried to hold back her giggling for a moment but then gave a piercing squeal of laughter. "How'd you know it was me, Owi?" she asked. Seri had recently taken to shortening the names of her family members because she decided her full name, Seridyn, was too long.

"Ma or Da wouldn't throw paper darts at me," Owin said, playing along.

"I learned how in school. My best friend showed me how," Seri said brightly and giggled. "She threw one at the school mistress, and she got mad, but mistress didn't know who threw it, so no one got in trouble."

"Let me show you how to fix these darts, so they fly longer." Owin pulled the closest dart onto his lap, and Seri stood up on his mattress, throwing her arms around his neck to see over his shoulder. The small weight of her body leaning against his back was warm and comforting.

As she watched him make a flap at the end of one of the dart's wings, she nonchalantly announced, "Ardyn taught me a new swear word."

Owin grinned up at her. "What is it today?"

"A-zor-e-an," Seri said, drawing out the unfamiliar word.

"Azorean," Owin said, and Seri repeated it to herself under her breath a few times. "It's not really a bad word, it's . . ." Owin paused, trying to decide how best to explain the complex idea to a child. "It's a name for people who live in the Middle Realm, the canyon that divides the Northern and Southern Realms." Owin decided against telling his little sister Azoreans had once been ordinary men and women until they unexpectedly came down with hard gray patches on their skin, a disease with no cure and thought to be the cause of the Fall of Edean. They then were instantly shunned and hated by everyone, which was why they all lived together in the Middle Realm, away from everyone else.

"Oh," Seri said, looking slightly crestfallen.

"Where did Ardyn hear it?" Owin asked.

"From an older boy in class," Seri said, and he could tell she'd lost interest in the word, as it wasn't one she could add to her growing collection of curse words. Owin finished the improvements to the dart and handed it to his sister. She inspected the changes with a critical eye before throwing the dart into the air. It flew straight for a moment, then turned into two complete loops before reaching the floor. Seri gave a laugh, leapt off Owin's bed, and, pouncing on the dart, ran out of the room

Owin lay back down and closed his eyes again before Seri's voice came through the door, sing-song and cloyingly sweet. "Owin! Your true love is here!"

Owin sat up and began to pull on his boots, wondering who it could be. He hadn't really been serious with anyone since Meda last summer, and her family had moved away. He tucked in his shirt and ran a hand through his unkempt brown hair, wishing his room had a mirror. He glanced about the room for anything out of place on the off chance he could convince his visitor to a private chat. Seeing nothing horrible out in the open, he walked out of his room, down the short hallway to the front room of the house, which held the large table for guests and visitors.

Owin put on what he considered his most charming grin and entered the room. Seri perched bird-like on one of the lacquered high-backed chairs around the table, next to a girl with long hair the color of ripe corn who was bent over the table, writing in a small leather- bound book.

Seri, who gleefully watched her older brother enter the room, opened her mouth to announce his presence, but he beat her to it, saying, "Hello and welcome—" The girl looked up, and the words died on Owin's lips.

It was only Brigid Dorcas, the librarian's daughter, a one time classmate of Owin's. She smirked over her notebook at him before resuming her writing. "Thank you for that gracious welcome, Owin. I hadn't expected to see you up and about during the morning hours."

Owin stood where he was for a moment, suddenly unsure of himself. There always seemed to be an unspoken competition between them, though seeing her in his house for the first time made him feel distinctly wrong-footed. To give himself a moment to think, he sat down at the table opposite his still grinning sister. "To what do we owe this dubious pleasure?"

"I think that is the most intelligent thing I've ever heard you say, Owin," Brigid said, not looking up. "Your father requested some old books on Southern law, so here I am." Two thick books with faded titles sat on the tabletop in front of Seri, whose eyes flicked back and forth between her brother and Brigid as if she were watching a game of Loft. "You do remember books, don't you? Hard, square things, filled with knowledge?"

"Oh that's what those are," Owin retorted. "I thought you just used them to stand on to make yourself taller."

Brigid, who had always been slightly shorter than other girls her age, pursed her lips together but didn't reply. She finished writing, slid the book in front of Owin, right side up, and held out her steel pen. "I'll need you to sign for these."

Owin took the pen and looked down at Brigid's tiny, concise writing. Both titles were listed, along with that day's date and his own name. Owin scrawled his name next to each title and passed the book and pen back across the table. Brigid scooped them up and slid both into a little pouch hanging from her belt. "How's the book lending business?"

"The same as ever, not too many recent advances in the art of lending," Brigid said, pulling on her specially made book sacks. One went over her head and rested against one hip, then the other strap cut the other way across her chest, accentuating her bosom much more than her dress alone had. Both sacks were half-full, though Owin was sure they were still heavy. "How is the loafing-about-and-not-doing-anything-with-your-life business going?"

"Very well, thank you," Owin said. "You'll be happy to know I am giving a wide variety of trades careful consideration."

"Oh, I didn't know staying out late with the town strumpet was a trade," Brigid said tartly.

"Is that jealousy, Miss Dorcas? And Gisel is hardly a strumpet."

"Jealousy? Don't make me laugh!" Brigid said, stopping at the front door and turning to face Owin. "As much as I like Vridian Ford, I don't plan to be stuck here, large with child and forced to live with my parents as Gisel and some others are destined to do. I want to go out and see all of Irillia and do something of importance!" The determination and fierceness in

Brigid's voice surprised Owin, and he bit back the joke he was about to make.

Instead, he said, "So I'll have to find someone else to have these rousing conversations with."

Brigid smiled slightly, and her voice lost its bite. "I suppose you will. I'll be sure to send some applicants your way." She turned to go out and nearly collided with Samuel Cadmon, mayor of Vridian Ford, who was entering at the same moment.

"I'm sorry, Brigid: I nearly knocked you over," Samuel said, stepping to the side once through the door.

"That'd be pretty hard to do with all the extra weight I have," Brigid said, patting one of the bags at her side.

Samuel raised an eyebrow. "Did you deliver the law books? That was very fast!"

"It wasn't any trouble," Brigid said, hooking her thumbs through the bag straps. "Well, I need to keep delivering." She gave Samuel a brief nod before hurrying through the door.

"Be sure to thank your father for me!" Samuel called after her and pulled the big front door shut.

Seri leapt off her chair, nearly knocking it over, and ran to her father. "Fa Fa!" she said, throwing her arms around his leg.

Samuel lifted her up into the air. "How's my Ser Ser today?" He held her close, and they rubbed noses, sending Seri into a gale of giggling. As she began telling her father all about her time at school that day, Owin decided it would be the best time to slip away unnoticed. He loved his father but didn't look forward to having to listen to a lecture and was keen to put it off as long as possible.

Owin got up and walked unconcernedly toward the hallway leading to his room, but, before he'd taken more than a few steps, Samuel called out, "Owin! I'd like to have a word."

When he was younger, Owin might have taken off at a run, daring his father to catch him before he listened to anything, and, while he still felt a slight desire to do so, he turned and saw both Samuel and Seri staring at him; his father looked thoughtful and Seri wore an eager grin as she waited for her older brother to get into trouble.

"Ser Ser, I want you to go into your room and make me one of those paper darts," Samuel said, setting her on the floor. Seri nodded vigorously and scurried past her older brother to disappear into her own bedroom.

Samuel picked up the two borrowed books from the table and held them under one arm as he approached Owin. "Son, I wanted to know if you decided on a trade you wanted to pursue."

Not expecting this to be the topic of conversation, Owin hid his surprise to meet his father's gaze for a moment before looking away. "I haven't decided." He cast about for the first job he could think of, just to gauge his father's reaction, something he had tried several times before. "I might go to Alewor and enroll in the army."

Samuel frowned slightly. "I really think you should aim a bit higher than that. You're a bright lad; I know you were just behind Brigid in marks at school."

"Not too hard to do with only five others our own age."

Samuel did not smile at this but continued to stare at his son until Owin felt as if his steady gaze was about to burn a hole through him, scorching the wall behind him. They both shared the same dark blue eyes, but Owin didn't think he'd ever manage a stare half as intense as his father's. "I wish you'd reconsider following in my footsteps. If you clean up your act now and start attending village councils, you'd have a real shot in eight or ten years."

Owin tried and failed to keep sarcasm out of his voice. "Is that all? Ten years of attending monotonous council meetings for a chance to lead more monotonous council meetings?"

His father clenched his jaw for a moment before speaking, a warning sign Owin knew too well. "The Council can be a bit formal and tedious, yes, but it is where all decisions are made, and it is a responsibility I bear proudly." Samuel reached out and laid a hand on his son's shoulder. "It is far past time you took on some responsibility and thought of the good of others, not just yourself."

Owin met his father's steady gaze for a moment before shifting his attention to the bridge of his father's nose, a trick he'd picked up in school so as not to become uncomfortable. "Yes, I do have to take more responsibility, but I can do that in work other than being on the Council."

"Very true, but you need to pick something. We've had this discussion at least half a dozen times since you finished school. You need to make a decision and stick with it. I expect to hear your choice by the end of the week, or we will be having a very different conversation. Do you understand?"

Samuel had never struck any of his children, and Owin was too old now for that kind of punishment, so he merely nodded. Samuel clapped him on the shoulder once and continued down the hall to Seri's room.

Owin remained where he was for a moment, his thoughts jumbled. He had four days to make a decision, something he was sure he could do in less time. Owin actually had his choices narrowed down to a bare handful.

He walked down the hallway and, by the time he stepped into his room, Owin made up his mind he would announce his choice tomorrow and show his father he could be decisive. Owin also decided, as it had been over a fortnight since he last visited the *Green Barrow*, Darrt's Field's only inn, he was overdue for his next visit. Darrt's Field was the next town south along the Oak Road, and, while the trip would take him the better part of an hour on foot, the journey would be worth it.

Owin scrounged about in his room until he uncovered three silver stags, more than enough to cover a meal and a few mugs of the inn's finest brew. He pulled on his second finest coat, trimmed with silver thread at cuffs and collar, walked out into the hall and pulled his bedroom door closed. As he was planning to return that night, he didn't pause at his sister's room to say good bye.

Owin walked outside onto the rock edged path that connected his front door with his neighbor's and headed for the village green. He nodded to the few townsfolk he passed and, as he crossed the wide expanse of short green grass, he began to feel a dull ache in his head, just over both ears. He experienced his share of such aches before, so he didn't give it much thought. The pain wasn't severe enough to warrant choking down one of old Mother Malkin's vile-tasting healing teas.

Owin passed by the open front door of the Unbroken Church, a low building of whitewashed stone, when he heard a voice calling his name from within. He turned back and saw his friend Taim Uturu, dressed in the white garb of a Church Cleric, emerge from the doorway. "Taim? Won't your mother be upset you cut up her best bed linen?"

Taim, a year or so older than Owin and stocky with very short red hair, held out his arms, so the long white sleeves pooled at his elbows. "Very funny, Owin. The Cleric was called away to some important gathering of Church leaders in the Citadel, so he left me in charge of the Eternal's House."

"That was nice of him, as he's your father and all. Why aren't you wearing the necklace?"

Taim looked slightly incredulous. "I've only been studying for a year; I've no right to wear the Unbroken Circle." He touched the large metal circle mounted on the front door of the church reverently. The circle was made of thin silvery metal, twisted in a way to make it appear as if it only had one edge.

"So, why aren't you just wearing a flour sack instead of actual Cleric garb?"

"Well, I have to look the part, don't I? Besides, flour sacks are not at all comfortable next to the skin," Taim admitted.

"Well, I'm glad you're not a full Cleric yet; otherwise, I'm sure I'd be in for a lecture about why I haven't set foot in the church for months."

Taim glanced about to see if anyone was within earshot and said, "Between us, so long as you have an occasional conversation with Him," he jerked his thumb upwards as if the Eternal Himself was sitting just overhead, "that's all that really matters."

"Exactly!" Owin said, rubbing at both of his temples with his fingers.

Taim glanced at the motion. "Head hurting?"

"Yes, just started a moment ago. Gotten a bit worse, actually." Owin felt as if his kneading fingers were doing some good, so he kept at it. "I was actually just on my way to the *Barrow*, if you can get away for a while."

Taim shook his head ruefully. "Someone must always be available in the church. Besides, if I am going to be a Cleric, I need to stop going to taverns."

"I suppose any girl who sits on your knee will slide right off." Owin felt at the slipperiness of the fabric of Taim's robe with two fingers.

"What about you, Owin? Decided on a trade yet?"

Owin grimaced slightly. "I've got it down to three choices. I'm going to tell my father my decision tomorrow."

Taim clapped him on the shoulder. "Good man. So this'll be your farewell trip to the *Barrow*?"

"Something like that," Owin said, and stopped kneading his temple for it seemed to no longer help. The pain had increased again, and Owin considered for a moment not going to the *Green Barrow* at all, but then stubbornly resolved to go, pain or no, when he thought again of the ultimatum his father had delivered. "Well, I'd best start off if I want to get there before the drunks wake up."

"Enjoy!" Taim said cheerfully and walked a few paces back inside the church before turning back. "If you feel the need to get rid of some guilt tomorrow over the things you'll do tonight, feel free to stop by!"

Owin chuckled to himself, raised a hand in farewell and continued on his way. Vridian Ford had no physical boundary; so far as he knew, no fences or row of stones marked the village limits, though he was sure his father knew down to the yard what land was considered part of his town.

There weren't many folk on the Oak Road; Vridian Ford was nowhere near either of the two major cities of the Northern Realm, so the roads connecting small towns usually were only used by locals. The early autumn weather was fine, the wind carrying the barest bite of cold.

Owin continued on for nearly half an hour; the pain in his head was as constant as his shadow, which often merged with the denser shadows at the edge of the road cast by overhanging boughs. The pain spiked suddenly, making Owin feel as if a red hot nail was being driven into each temple. His vision began to darken at the edges, and his only thought, crawling against the pain as if up a steep mountain slope, was to get off the road.

He stumbled sideways, dimly aware of bushes scraping against his boots and tugging against his pants. He doggedly continued forward, hoping to find a nice, cool tree trunk to lean against, when his foot caught on something, and he sprawled forward. His head struck something only slightly softer than a smith's anvil and, with a bright pop of light behind his eyelids, the excruciating pain—and everything else—vanished into blessed darkness.

Chapter 2

Brigid pushed open her kitchen door to find her mother, Iona, seated at the round table in the center of the small room, bent over a single sheet of paper and writing in her elegant hand with a short steel pen. Books covered most of the table, many of them lying open to a specific page.

Brigid hung her empty book sacks on a peg by the door, and her mother said, "Thank you, darling." She did not look up from her work, save to dip the quill in an inkwell lying open at her elbow. The bright nib of another pen could be seen in the midst of a tidy bundle of hair resting on the back of her head. "Can you put the kettle on? I've already set out the tea things."

"Of course," Brigid said, after a slight hesitation, knowing the only time her mother asked her to make tea was when there was something important to discuss. Brigid moved around the table to the small hearth and shifted the coals around with the poker, allowing the fire to grow a bit before swinging the small teapot on the iron arm over the flames. "What are you working on?" Brigid asked, replacing the poker.

"A new deed for the Kildare farm. They've bought up a smaller one to use for a pasture, and the finer details are a bit tricky as the boundaries are marked differently on older maps."

Brigid smiled to herself as she looked at the spread of books on the table. The deed must have been tricky indeed if her mother had brought books into the kitchen. Usually it was the one room in their small house she kept clear of books, as she often said the notion of having books in every room of the house would be enough to drive her to drink.

Iona set down her pen so the nib balanced over the open rim of the inkwell, blotted and sanded the paper, before sliding it carefully into a velvet-lined portfolio. She then cleaned the nib of her pen with an ink-stained cloth, taking much more time and care than Brigid normally did with her own. However, Brigid knew this was a means her mother sometimes used to buy more time to think, particularly on delicate or important conversations.

The sound of boiling water pulled her gaze from her mother, and she swung the teapot on its arm away from the fire, before scooping in two spoonfuls of dried, crushed tea leaves from the battered tin jar on the mantle. The kitchen filled with the warm aroma of mint and apple as she stirred the tea before leaving it to steep.

Iona piled up most of the books on the table into a bundle, and Brigid moved to stack up the rest as her mother left the kitchen with her first armload. Iona returned a moment later and took the other stack from her daughter. Brigid knew she must have merely set them on an empty shelf in the hall to be sorted later.

Using the hem of her dress to shield her hands, Brigid lifted the teapot and poured two cups of tea, careful to strain out as many of the leaves as she could. Brigid brought the two cups of faded white pottery to the table, even as her mother returned and brought over the small pot of honey from the shelf by the closed pantry door. Iona always took her tea black, though she kept a supply of honey on hand for Brigid, who disliked the bitterness of plain tea.

Brigid stirred a generous portion of honey into her tea, watching the dark liquid lighten as she waited for Iona to begin.

"Do you know I heard there is a new practice in the Southern Realm called 'reclaiming tea?' It involves gathering up used tea leaves, thoroughly drying them and adding a dusting of powdered copper to turn the leaves green. It sells for a quarter of what new tea costs, but I'm sure it must taste ghastly."

Brigid blinked at her mother, teaspoon held motionless in her hand. Iona, easily the most well-read in the entire village, often shared random bits of information in everyday conversation, but it was hardly what Brigid was expecting to hear. Iona smiled and said, "I tell you this because I was going to ask if you wouldn't mind going into the Southern Realm for some deliveries, and I don't want you drinking any reclaimed tea; all that copper can't be good to drink."

"I don't mind at all; would I be going to the capitol?" Brigid sipped at her tea and, deciding it wasn't sweet enough, reached for the honey again.

Iona nodded. "Yes, though there'll be a few other stops before Barwick." She curved her hands around her cup and studied her only daughter for a moment. "This will be your first time out on your own, so I also wanted to share some advice."

Brigid smiled slightly and nodded for her mother to continue, trying to prepare herself for anything she might chose to give advice on.

"The best way to discourage a man who won't take no for an answer is to strike hard and fast at his eyes with your nails. Most men will expect you to aim at a different spot on their body, so it will surprise them."

Brigid felt her cheeks warming and not from the tea. Iona studied her nails for a moment, and Brigid saw some were bitten, a habit her mother had while concentrating on a difficult task. "It's best to keep your nails longer, so as to be more effective."

"Thank you for that advice, Mother; I'll be sure to make use of it if necessary," Brigid said, desperately trying to come up with another topic of conversation.

"While we're on the subject of discouraging men, have there been any village boys you've said 'no' to lately?" Iona grinned, "or yes, for that matter?"

"Mother!" Brigid felt her cheeks flushing again. "I'm not—there is— I'm not going to talk to you about that!"

"You can share as many or as little details as you'd like." Iona leaned closer to her daughter, the tea momentarily forgotten on the table. "Mind, all I'm asking is if I need to start making an evergreen arch." Even the most casual follower of the Eternal knew an arch of evergreen boughs was one of the components of a traditional wedding ceremony in the Unbroken Church.

"No! No . . . not for a while yet." Brigid sipped at her tea to give herself something to do, so she wouldn't have to look at her mother's grin.

"I was married when I was only a year older than you are, and I'd already known your father nearly four years. There must be some nice young men you know who might be good husband material. What about the mayor's son?"

"No, absolutely not!" Brigid tried to keep her voice from rising to a squeak. "He's far too in love with himself and lazy to boot."

"I seem to remember them all being that way when I was your age," Iona commented.

"Anyway," Brigid said with a touch of asperity, "I want to have things done before I marry, things that might be too hard to do as a wife and mother."

"Such as?"

"I don't know, maybe writing a book. I've always wanted to write one."

"Do you have an idea in mind?"

"No, not yet," Brigid admitted. "I want it to be about something important. I'll know it when it comes."

"Maybe you could write one about the dangers facing young women who wait too long to find a husband."

"Finding a husband is not the solution to all of life's problems, Mother," Brigid said. "I'm sure there are many unmarried women who lead full, happy lives." Brigid couldn't think of any in Vridian Ford, but she was confident there had to be someone *somewhere* in Irillia.

"No, you're right. Marriage solves some problems, but then more spring up to take their place." Iona set down her empty teacup and placed her hand over her daughter's free hand resting on the table. "I just worry sometimes you're so busy, chasing these ideas and dreams, you'll forget time is passing you by."

"There's no chance of that with you reminding me every other day."

"It's been at least a week, and you know it." Iona said, effecting a sniff of indignation, but then she smiled, somewhat spoiling the effect. "All right, enough is enough for one day." Iona pulled her purse off of her belt and counted out a short stack of silver stags onto the table before her daughter. "I'd like you to be off early tomorrow morning. There's enough coin there for you to stay at an inn every night on your trip, but I want you to try to avail yourself of the hospitality of any village librarians you encounter; Eternal knows I've given room and board to enough of them on their travels."

Brigid nodded and scooped the small stack of coins into her purse. "Will I be picking anything up or just delivering?"

"Just delivering. This year has been quite slow for book borrowing in Vridian Ford; I can't understand why."

Brigid did not care to get into another discussion; she was very much looking forward to being out on her own at last to waste time in idle speculation. She considered it likely her mother would try to work the idea of marriage into the conversation somehow, and she'd had enough on the topic to not even want to *think* of the word for the next year. "I'll get started packing."

Iona smiled fondly at her daughter. "Should take you less than a quarter of an hour, how organized your room is."

Brigid returned her mother's warm smile as she rose from the table. "I learned from the best."

"Flattery will only get you everywhere; that's why it's so easy," Iona said, though Brigid could tell she was pleased in spite of her words. Brigid left the kitchen, new found responsibility and the prospect of leaving Vridian Ford for a bit making her happy in equal measure.

Chapter 3

Owin's first realization as he woke was the lack of
mind-numbing pain. There was a twinge of discomfort in the
cheek he was lying on, but it was so much less painful than the
thunderstorm in his skull had been, he barely noticed it. He
slowly sat up and opened his eyes, though only one seemed able.
He gingerly touched the one not opening and found it crusted
shut with dried blood. Owin was able to wipe enough of it away
to open his eye, but he could still feel a patch of dried blood on
his cheek that wouldn't come off, despite vigorous scrubbing. It
would have to wait until he could get in front of a mirror or, at
least, the horse trough in front of the *Green Barrow*.

Sweat dripped down his forehead and already soaked
through his shirt, and he felt as though he'd just gotten over an
intense bout of the chills. He had no idea what had come over
him, perhaps an intense head cold; however, at the moment, all
he cared was   it was over. Owin could still see sunlight filtering
down through the trees, so he figured he'd been out for no more
than a few hours.

Owin pulled himself to his feet, straightened his clothes
as best he could and looked for the Oak Road, as he had no idea
from what direction he came from. He could see the trees
thinning out half a dozen yards from where he stood, so he

headed in that direction, watching where he stepped as he had no wish to have a twin bruise on his other cheek. The Oak Road felt solidly reassuring under his feet, even though it was only hard packed dirt, and he continued on his way to Darrt's Field as though nothing had happened.

He was worried over how quickly he fell sick and then seemingly became well again; perhaps he would stop at the herb woman's house in the village after having at least one drink at the *Barrow.*

Owin didn't see anyone else on the road, even though there was at least a couple hours of sunlight left, judging by the position of the sun. He soon saw the wide arch spanning the entrance to Darrt's Field in the distance, so he quickened his pace. His stomach grumbled, and he decided he would also have a meal with his drink before seeking out the healing woman.

As he drew closer to the arch, he could see the large stones composing it, supposedly carted in from all over Irillia, from the Pearl Islands to the far south and the Drannon Desert far to the east. Those stones from the Islands were black as shadows at midnight and smooth as glass, and he ran his fingers across one as he passed through the arch before entering the village proper.

The closest shopkeepers to the arch were closing up for the day, three shops in a row all sharing one long roof. A pair of boys ran across the main street further ahead, tossing a ball between them before disappearing down a side street. A young woman, perhaps a year or so older than he, wearing a high-necked dress clung pleasantly to her figure, came around the corner towards him and, before they passed each other, Owin put on a wide smile.

While they were still a yard or so apart, the woman noticed him and came to a full stop, her eyes widening and her mouth opening, though no sound came out. "It's just a bit of blood, I—" Owin began, but the girl turned and ran back the way she came, as quickly as if a pack of wolves nipped at her heels.

Owin thrust his hands deep into his coat pockets, feeling off-balance for the second time that day, as if he'd been walking the edge of a precipice, and at any moment would lose his footing. He tried to brush it off before reaching the *Green Barrow*. He didn't see anyone else before he reached the inn, save two men who disappeared inside ahead of him, when he stopped by the horse trough in front of the vacant hitching posts. Using handfuls of cool water that smelled of hay and horse, he tried in vain to scrub away at the rest of the dried blood plastered to his cheek, but it stubbornly clung to his skin.

Refusing to let anything else ruin his last visit to the inn, he slicked his wet hair back off his forehead and pushed through the brightly painted green front door of the inn. He walked down a short hallway, passing a staircase leading up to the rooms for rent and finally reached the common room, pausing at the open door to take it all in. Long rows of low tables filled the room, all leading in straight lines to the large unlit fireplace at the front. The common room was fuller than he expected with perhaps fifteen patrons already seated and tucking in to heaping plates or nursing a mug or three. Pipe smoke already filled the air, and he took a deep breath of it; wishing he remembered his own pipe.

Owin spotted the innkeeper near the back of the room and began to walk down the nearest aisle between the long tables towards him. He glanced at what the men around him were eating, so he could have his order ready. A large hand roughly grabbed his wrist and spun him around, bringing him face to face with a broad-shouldered man with a short black beard and strong drink fumes on his breath. Before Owin could do more than open his mouth, the man stepped closer to him, the stink of sweat and beer filling Owin's nostrils, the man peering through bleary red eyes at Owin's face. "You got somefink all over your face, boy. You got somefink catching?"

"Yes, friend, just clumsiness." He moved to shoulder past the drunk, but the man still clamped onto his wrist, and a light of recognition flared suddenly in the man's eyes. He wrenched his hand from Owin's wrist as though scalded.

"You're a filthy Azorean!" The man's voice was much louder now.

Owin laughed nervously as he looked to the nearby tables to see if anyone had heard the man's pronouncement. "You've had a bit too much of the drink, friend. I'm not—"

"Azorean! Azorean! Azorean!" The man bellowed, backing away from Owin and jabbing an accusatory finger. All around Owin, heads turned and conversation cut off as if severed by an axe. A serving woman, who had been in the process of handing a full tankard to an impatient patron, screamed and dropped it. The mug clattered on the table, showering the nearest patrons with mead, but no one paid attention. The entire common room was silent now, all eyes on Owin.

He forced a large grin and held up his hands. "I am not a Azorean, friends!" Despite the lunacy of the situation, Owin could still detect a hint of hysteria in his own voice. "I can assure you all—" Owin broke off in mid-sentence, suddenly seeing the back of his right hand. Hard gray patches adorned his skin, as if he had worked with clay and allowed the residue to dry on his hands, forming irregular shapes. He lifted his other hand and saw the same gray blotches, though in a slightly different pattern.

A sharp blow to the side of his head jarred him back to the predicament he was in. Owin raised his hand to his right temple and felt a warm wetness trickling down the side of his face. "Filthy Azorean!" a man from a nearby table yelled.

Another sharp blow to the back of his head snapped Owin's neck forward. He saw flashes of light burst in front of his eyes, as well as a sudden, tremendous rage he had never felt before. The room filled now with angry shouts from all sides, and several men were on their feet, shaking fists at him. Owin felt anger growing inside him like steam trapped in a kettle until he felt something shift within his mind like a vent opening, and all the rage streamed through.

Out of the corner of his eye, he saw something small flying towards his head, and he instinctively flung up his hands to shield his face. Instead of colliding with his hands, the empty mug changed direction in mid-air as if bouncing off an invisible wall. The mug clattered to the floor several feet away, and Owin stared at it for a moment, confused. He looked up just in time to see two more empty mugs arcing toward him from different directions. Owin crouched down, arms over his head, and the cups fell within a few inches of him before suddenly veering off course.

Owin stood back up and saw three burly men, each at least a head taller than he, reaching towards him with thick arms.

He stepped up onto a nearby vacant bench and then up onto the table, knocking over a few mugs abandoned by their owners. The volume of shouting and hurled insults increased as he ran down the length of the table. Owin caught sight of the innkeeper, now shaking his fist and mouthing words that were lost in the commotion.

Owin's booted feet thumped down hard on the stone floor as he reached the end of the table, and he pushed roughly past a few newcomers at the door, tore down the hallway and burst through the front door of the inn. His only thought was to get as far away from those men as possible before they decided it had been too long since the village's last lynching.

Owin turned right on the first cross street past the inn and kept running. Lamps on tall iron poles lined the length of the street, not yet lit by men balancing expertly on tall stilts, and he chanced a glance over his shoulder at the inn. No one had followed him out into the street yet, but he did not slow his pace. He soon came to the last building at the end of the street and rounded the far corner of the building before letting himself stop.

Owin looked down at his hands in the late afternoon sunlight and slowly curled them into fists as the full reality of his situation crashed down like a falling tree. His belly roiled violently, even though he hadn't eaten a thing since morning, and he felt a scream building up in this throat, desperate to be let out. Not wishing to draw any attention to himself, he punched the wooden side of the building next to him as hard as he could.

All this accomplished was pain in his knuckles. The skin on one finger had split, and a slow trickle of blood was oozing across his still clenched fingers, though he barely noticed. Owin sank down to a seated position, back against the wall, hugging his knees to his chest. It was not exactly cold out, but the late afternoon air had a definite chill that was not blunted by the setting sun. As he sat huddled against the wall, he tried to recall a time when he felt so miserable, but he could not. The troubles he encountered at home from his parents or others in the town paled in comparison to this calamity.

Owin's thoughts were so absorbed he did not hear the quiet footfalls approaching the spot where he sat and so was taken by surprise to feel a hand fall on his shoulder. He looked up, tensing, prepared to see one of the angry mob from the common room, and he was surprised to see the person standing over him. She was a young woman with red hair, about his own age, and her face was covered in scaly gray patches. Owin was so surprised to see an Azorean standing brazenly in the middle of Daart's Field, he barely registered the fact she was wearing a dark colored cloak which blended easily into shadow over a simple brown dress.

She stared down at him for a moment, and then her face broke into a wide grin. "Welcome, brother. My name is Meryl." She bent down and placed her hands around Owin's upper arms, pulling him to a standing position. Owin could think of nothing at all to say, so he just stared down at her. "I know what you're feeling right now; I went through it myself only a year ago. Let me assume you just Changed?"

Owin forced his voice past a large lump in his throat. "What?"

"It is what we Azoreans call the time when a person's skin breaks out in patches, and they first manifest their Talent, if they have one." She must have seen the question form on his lips; she elaborated. "Leon says it is 'the compensation the Eternal gives all Azoreans in exchange for their isolation'."

Owin took in very little of what this young woman just said, but he met her gaze at the mention of the word *Azorean*. "So it's true . . . I really am an . . ." Owin's voice trailed away before he could bring himself to say the word aloud. As foolish as it seemed, Owin felt he could hold on to a small shard of hope if he didn't say the word out loud, so he held that to his breast with a grip of iron. "I haven't noticed anything odd about myself recently," Owin said, trying to bolster his words with nonchalance.

"Other than patches of your skin turning gray and hard?" Meryl asked, the corners of her mouth turning up slightly. "If it hasn't happened yet, it will soon. Once an Azorean's skin turns, a Talent, if there is one, is never far behind."

"What is your Talent?" Owin asked, wondering if she was about to describe the strange occurrence that happened in the common room.

"I can see and hear things no one else at distance can. If I concentrate, I can see a fly folding its wings at twenty paces or hear a mouse cough on the next street over."

Owin stared at her for a moment in silence before realizing his mouth was open slightly. What she just said was absurd, but less so than the idea that he was— His mind skipped over the word, refusing to acknowledge it. "So every one of your kind has a different Talent? I've never heard of that."

"Not all Azoreans have a Talent. There's a lot that Irillians don't know about us. No one can seem to get over our appearance or the fear of becoming one of us themselves, even though we're not contagious. Azoreans have a wide variety of Talents, and there are some who share the same kind of Talent. A few have been blessed with two."

"Like you?" Owin could not help but stare at her eyes. In the low light, it was hard to tell the color, but he thought they

might be a pale shade of blue. Her eyes looked to be the same
size and shape as any other pair Owin had seen, though she still
wore her hood up so he could not see if her ears were larger than
normal.

"Yes, like me. Because of my Talents, I am often sent
out of the Colony on different errands, sometimes just to look
for Azoreans who just Changed."

"Are there that many of you?"

"There are more than a hundred of us back at our Colony.
I don't find many new Azoreans, maybe one every couple of
months, but there are several of us out looking all the time. Now
I've found you, you are welcome to return with me to the
Colony." Meryl paused for a moment, cocking her head to the
side, as the old Cadmon family dog used to when trying to catch
an elusive sound. "Someone just opened a door a few buildings
down. Let's get under cover before anyone sees." She turned
away from the nearby street and walked towards the back of the
building Owin had leaned against, towards a line of shadow-clad
trees that must have marked the edge of town.

Owin stared after her retreating form for a moment
without following. His mind lay adrift in a sea of conflicting
thoughts, and he knew if he went after her, it would be one step
closer to accepting tonight's events as his new life. For a
desperate moment, he hoped he could make it home to Vridian

Ford and maybe stay hidden away indoors for the rest of his life; he then realized, while his family would take pity on him, no one else in the village would. His family would become instant pariahs, because of him. Owin's vision blurred at the edges as tears slid down his face.

Meryl had nearly reached the line of trees when he wiped his face on his sleeve and hurried after her. The first step was hardest thing Owin had ever done in his entire life, and as he fell in step behind her, he kept his hands balled into fists at his sides to prevent them from shaking.

The pair walked in silence through the thickening trees; the only sounds were the gentle rustling of leaves overhead and the dry crunch of their fallen fellows beneath Owin's boots. They walked in single file with Owin concentrating on the backs of her boots, trying to push every other thought out of his mind but not succeeding.

The next few days were the longest and loneliest of his entire life, even though Meryl was usually only an arm's length away and friendly. With every step he took, he felt himself moving further and further from his old life towards one he never considered or wanted.

They traveled all day long and as far into the night as was feasible, staying to the woods and thickets as much as possible, crossing over dirt or cobble stoned roads only to plunge back into the wilderness on the other side. Owin had never been one for extended walks, and his legs soon began to protest in strident terms, but he found he could ignore them and the multiple blisters that formed on his feet by concentrating on the vast desert of his misery.

Meryl hunted as they walked, usually only needing one casually thrown knife from the brace of those she wore hidden away in various places over her body. She tucked the game away into a cloth sack that gradually bulged out at her hip as she added mushrooms, berries, or other plants to go with their meat at the evening's meal.

Owin began the journey tucked into the deepest corners of his mind that he could reach, feeling wretchedly sorry for himself and speaking only when absolutely necessary, ignoring all of Meryl's attempts at conversation. By the beginning of the third day, he began to feel the tiniest bit better, though his old life left a huge gaping wound he had no idea how to cover, let alone help to heal.

He found talking helped take his mind off his predicament, so he started talking about anything that came into his head, so long as it touched nowhere near his previous life. Meryl actively listened and responded with simple comments, seeming to understand the need Owin felt to distract himself, as well as knowing he neither wanted to talk about the Colony nor his recent Change.

Owin and Meryl traveled this way for several days, though much of it was a long blur to Owin as he barely took notice of when one day ended and the next began. He awoke one morning, a crick in his back from sleeping on a gnarled tree root he missed seeing in the dark, and Meryl announced they were less than a day's journey from the Colony.

As they drew closer, Owin discovered he actually looked forward to reaching the Colony, though he couldn't decide if it was from a desire to possibly find a place that could begin to fill the Vridian Ford-shaped hole in his life or because he was just sick of walking. His legs and feet no longer ached, but he was tired of the seemingly endless trek.

Even this close to the Colony, Meryl kept their path deeper in the trees away from the road, although they were still close enough to hear the occasional cart or horse go by in either direction, and their path seemed to run parallel to the road. As they had traveled through the trees and undergrowth for the vast part of their journey, Owin rather thought he had improved at moving quietly through the uneven terrain, though it was nothing compared to how softly Meryl could walk while still keeping the same pace.

Owin had crossed over the Middle Realm, the large canyon that almost completely separated both Realms of Irillia, a few times previously on the thick bridges that crossed the canyon as its narrow-most points but had not given much thought to what lay at the bottom. Now, he reflected as he followed Meryl down a series of stairs cut into the rock of the canyon wall; it made sense for the Azoreans to live in the Middle Realm for no one else really had reason to go down into its depths. The entrance to the stairs was covered in a thick, leafy bush with small yellow flowers scattered over its surface, though Meryl passed through it as if it were no more of a hindrance than a sheet of falling water. The bush proved much less yielding for Owin, and he left a scattering of petals on the ground in his wake.

Owin tried to keep count of the number of stairs but lost track somewhere after one hundred. As he descended, he tried to catch a first sight of the Colony, but the majority of what he could see of the floor of the canyon was obscured by greenery. Thick shrubs of various kinds sprouted out of the sides of the canyon at every imaginable angle, their long branches reaching out to neighboring bushes as if frozen in the act of greeting. The branches did not extend far enough to touch those on the other wall of the canyon; there was a span of at least thirty yards of empty air between them, but the greenery was still sufficiently thick enough to obscure his view of what lay below. He wondered if the Azoreans had specifically planted these bushes to protect their home from unfriendly eyes and was about to voice his question to Meryl when they passed one final turning of the stairs and came under the overhanging canopy of bushes. He caught sight of the cavern floor at last.

The edges of the canyon suddenly sprang away several yards as if all the dirt had been pulled away to widen the floor of the canyon, leaving the staircase completely free of external support. They were much closer to the canyon floor than Owin would have supposed with only two dozen or so steps to the ground. A cluster of small domes covered in green moss lay spread out in two large groups, one on either side of the staircase pillar, and larger buildings lay closer to the center of the canyon floor. These were of undressed gray stone and long rows of crops, being tended by several bare-chested men, surrounded the cluster of buildings.

On the other side of the crops were more of the small domed structures, clustered all the way up to the opposite wall of the canyon. A man and a woman, dressed in simple loose trousers and flowing white shirts, came up to the base of the stairs just as Meryl and Owin reached the rocky ground. The man was tall and strapping with thick arms and the dark skin of the Pearl Islanders. He wore a short bristling beard that left his upper lip bare, and his black eyes twinkled as he looked Owin over with an appraising glance, as if Owin were a piece of horseflesh the man might purchase. The woman was shorter, with black hair that ran down her back in waves. Her eyes were of two different colors, one as black as pitch, the other yellow as burnished gold. Owin had heard of folk possessing different colored eyes, so he wasn't sure if this was a result of her Talent.

No, it is not a result of my Talent, young man. The words formed in Owin's mind, seemingly of their own accord, with force that pressed on his ears as a sudden loud noise might. Owin stopped moving with one foot on the ground and his other on the last step, looking at the yellow haired woman. She met his gaze evenly without changing her expression of polite interest. The man next to her broke into a wide grin that took up half his face.

Meryl bowed her head, first to the woman and then to the man, before turning to grin at Owin. "Is something wrong, Owin?"

Before he could answer, words formed in his mind which were not his own, large and insistent. *Yes, please share what has you looking like a girl who has just been goosed for the first time in her life.* As soon as the last word formed in his mind, the large man gave a single bark of laughter.

"Come now, Telas. I think this is all surprise enough for this lad without you putting your thoughts into his head," the man said with the slight accent of the Pearl Islands which lengthened certain vowels. He extended his arm across to Owin, who grasped it and felt a grip stronger than iron. "Good to meet you, lad. I am Oxymandias, Ox for short. This beauty beside me is Telas." He pulled Owin close for a moment, nearly yanking his arm off. "Just between us, Telas and I are lovers. Wouldn't want you to hear that from anyone else first." Ox winked and patted Telas' backside, making no effort to hide this expression of endearment.

Telas winced slightly and said, "Oxen of my heart, I do wish you would remember what your prodigious strength can do to ordinary flesh."

"Who says I haven't, Telas, my love?" He winked at Owin again.

"Welcome to the Colony, Owin. I am Telas, and, between this brute and I, we are the leaders of the Colony." She arched an eyebrow at Ox.

Owin realized she was silently dressing the large man down with words in his mind, for Ox's eyes narrowed before he said, "Telas is in charge of the mundane, everyday concerns of running this place, while I am in charge of the defense of the Colony and all our topside excursions."

"Defense?" Owin said. "I thought this was a secret place."

"Aye, but it always pays to be prepared," Ox said with a grin.

"Tell us about yourself, Owin," Telas said.

"Couldn't you just read my mind?" Owin met her mismatched eyes and smiled.

"I would never presume to look into someone's mind without their permission." Telas' calm expression was marred only marginally by the slight upward curve of the side of her mouth. "Most of the time."

"I'm from Vridian Ford, a small town in the Northern Realm." Telas nodded as if she had heard of it before, though Ox did not give any sign of recognition.

"About a week ago, my head started hurting and wouldn't stop. I began to feel faint and passed out near the side of the road. When I came to, I felt much better and continued on to the inn I was visiting that day." Owin trailed off, remembering the looks of disgust, the hatred in every voice.

He felt Ox's strong grip on his shoulder for a moment and Telas said, "We've heard a similar tale from the lips of every new Azorean who comes to us. Did your Talent manifest then?"

Owin hesitated and then explained what happened with the cups. Telas looked thoughtful for a moment. "It sounds like your Talent may be moving objects with your mind, though I am not sure. This will be the first thing you do tomorrow after your morning meal. We will see if that is indeed your Talent and what control you have over it." Telas took Ox's arm and nodded to Meryl. "Meryl will show you to your assigned hut and where to report tomorrow morning. Until then, Owin." Ox winked again and smiled, and the pair walked away towards the fields.

While they talked, Owin observed several Azoreans walk past on various tasks or errands. They all wore clothing similar to Ox and Telas, always in muted colors. Owin saw both men and women of various ages, from about his own age to those whose hair was pure white, what there was of it. There were no children in sight, and Owin recalled the affliction that transformed normal people into Azoreans did not strike children.

"Follow me, Owin." Meryl started off along the outer row of the small green domes, walking parallel to the canyon wall. "What do you think of the Colony so far?"

"It's different than I pictured it," Owin admitted. "It seems to be very well organized."

"Did you think it would be a bunch of us rolling about in filth like pigs?" Meryl asked with a smile.

"No, not quite," Owin said and frowned slightly. "I've spent my whole life being taught to avoid Azoreans, that they are to be utterly despised, and, suddenly I— everything I've been taught about them is wrong."

"That's something else everyone who first comes to the Colony must deal with." Meryl stopped by a particular green dome, indistinguishable from its neighbors, save for a small wooden sign over the door, bearing the number 'eighty-nine'. "This will be your sleeping hut for now." She turned to look up at Owin. "I know this is a great deal to take in all at once; I know it was for me. I have other duties tomorrow, but I will see you at the morning meal." She reached up, cupped the side of Owin's face for a moment and smiled. "Sleep well. Don't worry during the night." Meryl let her hand fall and, turning, strode away through the green mounds.

Owin watched her walk away for a moment, his lips quirking slightly toward a grin. As he bent and pushed through the canvas covering the small doorway into the mound, he realized that was first time in days that he'd even felt like smiling.

Although he could not stand up once inside, there was more space than there appeared from the outside. A fern-stuffed mattress lay on the ground, complete with a pillow and wool blanket. A small chest sat open at the foot of the mattress, though Owin possessed no belongings to place within, and a filled pitcher and basin sat on the ground next to the chest. Owin pulled off his boots and sat on the edge of the mattress, looking around at his new home. Considering the past few nights he had spent sleeping out under the stars, sleeping with a roof over his head was a nice change. Owin lay down on the mattress, and the pillow under his head contained more lumps than he preferred, but he was tired enough not to care.

Chapter Four

Once Brigid crossed over one of the iron-banded wooden bridges spanning one of the narrower points of the Middle Realm, it was a journey of seven or eight days to Barwick, the capital of the Southern Realm. Fortunately, she was able to sleep in the library of the town or village she stopped at for the night. She was prepared to sleep under a bush or at the base of tree, despite the coin making a delightful weight in her purse; a yet untouched blanket roll was lashed under her saddle girth. The horse she brought out of Vridian Ford was a small gray mare with the unfortunate name of Mist, but, except for her name, the horse proved to be quite sensible and had a docile nature, which Brigid appreciated. She knew how to ride well enough; however, while the load of books was much lighter than what Mist was used to carrying, Brigid preferred to walk.

Brigid reached the capital just after stopping for a short midday meal, cresting a hill and suddenly seeing Barwick sprawled out before her. For Brigid, who was used to towns and villages being built alongside trees and undisturbed forests, it was quite a shock to see a massive cluster of white stone buildings with hardly a tree in sight. The city was entirely surrounded by a thick, tall white wall curved at the top, gleaming in the sun as if freshly whitewashed. Not only were there very few spots of green visible within the city walls, there were no trees whatsoever outside of the walls for at least a half a mile in every direction.

Brigid noticed several roads, some stone and others hard packed dirt, all converging from different directions and ending at a red brick road leading straight into the city. Steady streams of people were making their slow way in. Brigid often heard the people who lived in the Southern Realm rarely rushed or hurried but preferred to take their time doing things at their own pace. She took up Mist's reins and led her down the hill and onto the red brick road behind a merchant's large wagon loaded with small wooden casks. Almost immediately, three women carrying woven baskets overflowing with turnips came up behind Mist.

Brigid followed the merchant's wagon along the red brick road, watching the walls of the city grow steadily more massive with each step forward. They came to a halt some twenty yards from the arched entrance into the city, and Brigid could see a pair of guards speaking briefly to each wagon driver before waving them in.

Brigid spent the time studying the few people who passed her heading out of Barwick. The majority of them were Southerners, to judge from their clothes and stature. Those who lived in the South were generally shorter than Northerners and had slightly darker skin and hair. Their clothes, while cut in similar fashion and style, usually were of cloth dyed brighter hues than Northerners often wore.

Brigid came up to the pair of guards, noting the small silver sigil of the Southern Realm pinned to the right shoulder of each man. She expected them to raise a hand to halt her, but one guard just nodded to her, and the pair turned their eyes to the trio bearing turnips behind her.

She passed under the archway, admiring the highly polished and carved wood lining the arch. A pair of identical wooden doors rested open against both sides of the archway, each door almost two paces across and studded with iron bolts. The wall surrounding Barwick was not as thick as she supposed from the outside, and she soon emerged from a short tunnel onto a street only slightly less wide than the red brick road, paved with wide gray stones.

The street was lined with wooden stalls set cheek by jowl together and covered with cloth awnings in a variety of colors. The air was filled with the din of shopkeepers calling out their wares to the passersby, most of which paid them no mind. Conflicting smells assaulted her nose: horse dung, refuse, unwashed bodies and cooking meats. The majority of the people were heading deeper into the city, and, after a moment, Brigid followed their example.

At first, she tried to walk alongside Mist to keep an eye on the parcel of books, but Brigid soon realized there really wasn't enough room with the sheer number of people around her. So she resolved to walk leading her mount, glancing back frequently to make sure the leather buckles were still tightly closed. She realized also this act pointed her out as a newcomer to Barwick like nothing else would, but she had no intention of losing even one book.

At the first crossroad she came to, she took a left onto a much narrower street, lined with dirty storefronts, much more unkempt than those on the main street. Several blocks down, she took a right, and then another right. Brigid had come to a part of the city which was filled with stone buildings three and four stories tall, their faces marred, as if by pockmarks with small square windows fitted with dirty glass. The stone was white washed but had not seen a fresh coat of paint in at least ten years. Brigid knew the majority of Barwick's residents lived in apartments very similar to these buildings, whole families crammed into a single room.

A few streets further on, she found the library, a large, square building topped with a stone dome covered in faded bronze streaked with verdigris. She tied Mist's reins to a long hitching post in front of the library and swung the bulging saddlebags over her shoulder. Brigid patted Mist's sleek head, making a mental note to find some carrots for her.

Brigid spent much less time in the library than she expected, and less than an hour later, she walked out, her saddlebags considerably lighter than when she had gone in. Her mother told her before she left home not to count on the library having room to put her up for the night, and she was therefore not surprised when the Matron of the Library informed her the library had no spare beds. Brigid was secretly glad she had to find a room for rent, as she wanted a chance to experience what it was like to spend the night at an inn within a big city. Before she left the library, the Matron gave her a few silver coins and told Brigid they would be more than enough to buy a bed at a specific inn which was only a few blocks away called *The Queen's Ledger*.

The Matron claimed it was the cleanest and safest inn in the city, and not long after leaving the library, Brigid was speaking to the innkeeper of *The Queen's Ledger*. The man's name was Pynce, and he was very tall with fine wrinkles at the corners of his eyes and a small bald patch at the crown of his head, not much larger than one of the coins Brigid paid him. His white apron was immaculate and looked to be so starched Brigid expected to hear it crackle like paper every time he moved.

Pynce was soft spoken and had perfect pronunciation without a hint of the accent   usually common among Southerners. He summoned one of his serving men with a prodigiously loud snap from his thin fingers and instructed the young man who appeared to stable Mist. The young man, who had glossy black hair and high cheek bones, flashed a toothy smile at Brigid before hurrying away.

Master Pynce showed her to her room himself, carrying her mostly empty saddlebags stiffly at his side. The inn had a dozen rooms all on the second floor, and Master Pynce informed her only half the rooms were occupied. He bowed her into the room second on the left from the stairs. The room he had chosen was small and square with a bed set against the far wall. There was a small table with an empty pitcher and bowl and a stool tucked just beneath the table. Several wooden pegs were pounded into the wall opposite the table for hanging clothes, and a polished board lay across a few of the pegs, forming a makeshift shelf.

Master Pynce left after he informed Brigid the common room started serving dinner at dusk. Brigid unpacked a few things and hung her traveling cloak on a peg. She sat down on the side of the bed and was pleasantly surprised at the firmness of the mattress. The bed was not much wider than her own at home, and she was glad the inn was not at full capacity, for Iona had told her it was not uncommon for inns to sleep two or three to a bed.

With one last look around the room, she tied her money bag to her belt and firmly closed her door. The hallway was deserted, so Brigid took the stairs down to the first floor. She paused at the doorway to the common room. The room was large, filled with long tables; all vacant, but very clean. Empty fireplaces sat at both ends of the room, and candelabras dangled from the ceiling on short copper chains. A middle aged serving woman scraped out burned out candle stubs and replaced them with new, long-wicked candles. Brigid watched the woman for a few moments, then headed down the hallway and out the front door.

She had meant to walk around the city for an hour or two, perhaps to see what she could of the Viridian Keep, but she glanced up at the sky and saw the sun obscured by clouds, thick as a bale of wool; rain seemed imminent. Brigid wavered for a moment, watching the clouds and attempting to gauge if she had time to even make it a few blocks. She never had been good at telling the weather. Her father was one of the most respected experts on weather in Vridian Ford but had never been able to teach her much about reading clouds.

Brigid decided to stay close to the inn, and she strolled around the block, taking notice of the locals moving with purpose. Many she passed cast thoughtful looks up at the thickening clouds. A few small shops shared the same block as the inn, all cramped looking with windows of dirty glass. The only shop that looked at all prosperous was next to the inn. From the faded signs over the door, the shop proclaimed to be the oldest and most prestigious knife shop in all of Barwick.

She observed one vendor selling fruit from a shallow box looped about his neck with a bit of rope, and another vendor selling needles and pins set out on a round piece of wood covered in tattered black velvet. They were both slowly meandering in opposite directions, seeking shelter before the rain hit.

Brigid turned back onto the *Ledger's* street and saw a wooden coach parked on the other side with what appeared to be a large copper chimney poking incongruously through the roof. No horses stood in front of the coach; indeed, there was no wooden tongue protruding before the driver's seat where horses could be lashed. Brigid kept studying the strange coach as she walked up to her inn, and she paused just outside the front door for a longer look.

The driver's seat was recessed slightly back into the body of the coach with an overhang to keep the sun off the driver. Just in front of the seat was a wooden wheel, very similar to those used to steer ships, though she'd only ever seen pictures of those. Sprouting from beneath the wheel were a few metal levers at different angles like wilting flowers in a vase.

Despite the prospect of inclement weather, her curiosity was piqued so she crossed the street to get a better look. The sides of the coach wore a fresh coat of gray paint, still bright and slick. As she drew nearer, she could see two latches of polished copper and a pair of hinges outlining small doors on the side of the coach, one in front and one to the rear. The wagon's wheels seemed ordinary enough, save for a steel bar connecting the front and rear wheels together and one end disappearing up into the body of the carriage.

A man rounded the back of the wagon and nearly bowled her over in haste. Brigid barely even noticed his presence, much less had time to move out of his way, but the man sidestepped smoothly around her and turned, graceful as any dancer. "My pardon, miss," the man said, pulling off a thin gray cap and bowing his head slightly. "I am in need of some help with my steam carriage, and I wonder if you might oblige." He was dressed in a close fitting black coat and high boots, and his eyes could have been chipped from a frozen pond.

"Yes, if I can," Brigid found herself answering, silently berating herself for succumbing so easily to a pair of nice eyes. "Did you say 'steam', as in what's produced from boiling water?"

The man flashed a grin with very straight teeth. "Indeed, I did! Steam is going to be the new power driving our society, and it's cheaper than coal or wood until the King decides to start taxing water, that is." The man winked. "I am Creon Aldwulf, owner and currently sole employee of the Aldwulf Steam Company, though I'm hoping to expand very soon." Creon gave an elaborate bow, his left leg extended behind him.

"Nice to meet you, Master Aldwulf. I'm Brigid Dorcas," she said, inclining her head slightly, having no desire to try a curtsy as they invariably ended in disaster when attempted.

"Well met, Miss Dorcas. Just Creon, if you please; only my future employees need call me master." Creon winked again. "By your accent, I'd guess you are a Northerner?"

Brigid smiled slightly at this as she had drawn the same conclusion about Creon. "Yes."

"Right this way." Creon walked back around the rear of the carriage to the other side, which was identical to the opposite, save the steel rod connecting the two wheels on this side had slipped off the front wheel and lay on the cobblestones. He squatted down on his heels near the front wheel, and Brigid followed his example, careful to tuck the hem of her dress under her legs.

"It's a simple repair, though the connecting rod is quite heavy, and I can't lift it and hold the crank on the wheel in place at the same time." Creon indicated a short nub of metal sticking out of the side of the wheel. "Once I have it on, I just need you to slip this locking pin in place." He held up a long, thin cylinder of metal, similar to a steel bolt.

Brigid placed it on the cobbles by her feet and held the crank in place while Creon slowly lifted the connecting rod off the ground and fitted the circle of steel at the end over the crank. Brigid fitted the pin in place, and Creon hit it sharply with the palm of his gloved hand to make sure it wouldn't slip out.

He popped to his feet with a grin and held out his hand to help Brigid to her feet, but, as she had risen halfway already, she declined the offer. "Many thanks, Miss Dorcas. I was afraid I'd have to leave my invention here and return for it after the Unbroken Church had left the city."

Brigid wasn't sure what he meant; as far as she knew, the Church had been a presence in Barwick for as long as there had been a Barwick. Her uncertainty must have shown on her face because Creon said, "Every year a large group of Clerics of the Church makes a journey north from their Citadel to raise money and recruit new people to their faith. They are due to arrive in Barwick today, and they tend to hold a rather dim view of new things or progress in general, so I would most likely be thrown in prison for a few days while they're here."

"Just for creating something new?" Brigid asked, folding her arms as the wind picked up. "Do they really have that much influence with the King?"

"Yes, and not just in Barwick. They are on good terms with the House of Commons as well, so the local constabulary tends to turn a blind eye to all their doings, so long as it's not too far outside the law." Creon opened the small rear door on the side of the coach and did something to the inside, though Brigid's view was blocked by the open door.

A moment later, Brigid heard something *click*, and a thin tendril of steam began to unfurl from the chimney. Creon closed the door with a sharp *snap* and grinned at Brigid as he passed her on the way to the driver's seat. "I mean this in the best possible way, and I hope you won't take offense, but I do enjoy talking with small town folk. They have an innocence that is very refreshing."

Brigid paused a moment, trying and failing to parse the meaning behind his statement, so all she said was, "I see."

"I meant no offense, Miss Dorcas." Creon said, shifting two of the levers just beneath the ship's wheel. The steam issuing from the chimney thickened, and a low rumble of metal striking repeatedly on metal sounded from within the coach. "I thank you for your kind help. If ever I can be of service, the headquarters for my company is here in Barwick." Creon tipped his hat from where he sat and pulled a third lever. As the connecting rod elongated and withdrew into itself, the wheels shuddered and began to turn. The coach moved forward, not much faster than Brigid herself could walk but began to pick up speed as it turned the corner and disappeared from view.

Brigid remained where she stood for a moment, still indecisive about the meaning behind Creon's remark. She decided it didn't matter one way or another, as it wasn't likely she'd ever run into him again; she was intrigued, however, over this new use of steam as she previously thought its only use was to produce a sharp whistling sound when tea was ready. As she crossed the street to her inn, she thought she could remember seeing a book about the construction of horse-pulled wagons and coaches in her parent's collection back home. She decided to read up on the subject and see if she could work out how steam could be used to move something so large as a coach.

She pulled open the front door just as the first hesitant raindrops hit the cobbles behind her and heard several voices coming from the common room. Brigid paused at the common room door and saw perhaps a dozen men wearing various styles of clothing, sitting around one of the tables and were in the process of being served tankards of drink by a couple of serving maids. Brigid heard a small cough just behind her and turned to see Master Pynce standing with his hands clasped behind his back. "The common room shall be full early tonight, thanks to the inclement weather." The prospect of so many paying customers did nothing to change his expression. "I thought perhaps you might enjoy your time more in the quiet sitting room."

With a sweep of his arm, he indicated a closed door just opposite the entrance to the common room. Brigid opened the door to find a small room lit by a few candles in brass fixtures on the walls. Small mirrors set behind the flames magnified the light. An unlit fireplace, smaller than those in the common room and flanked by two bookshelves crammed with books, stood just opposite the door. A few small circular tables ringed with wooden armchairs took up most of the floor space. Brigid moved to the shelves to peruse the inn's collection, and Master Pynce said quietly, "I shall have one of the maids come and set a fire. Would you prefer to take your meal here?"

"Yes, thank you." Brigid turned to see Master Pynce bow himself out of the room. She turned her attention back to the bookshelf, recognizing several titles and authors from her family's modest collection. She ran her fingers over a row of spines and was pleased not to find a layer of dust.

At first glance, the books did not seem to be arranged in any particular order, and, as she moved on to the second bookshelf, this became more apparent. A rustle of skirts against the door frame made her turn around, and she saw a serving woman with her dark hair in a tight bun standing in the doorway. She smiled at Brigid and moved into the room, shielding a burning twig with one hand. She bent over the cold fireplace while Brigid turned back to the shelves. In a few minutes a small fire crackled away in the grate, and Brigid had decided how she wanted to organize the books. She began taking the books off the shelves and heard the serving maid announce to the room at large she would bring a dinner tray shortly.

Brigid lost herself in sorting the books, using all the small tables in the room for space. She was dimly aware of the mounting noise of the common room as it became more and more crowded, and once she fancied she heard a dull crack of thunder. When she was almost finished with one bookshelf, the handsome young serving man who had stabled Mist came into the library with an armload of wood.

Brigid had not noticed the fire had burned low, and the young man rebuilt the fire, all the while trying to catch her eye as he worked. She thanked him as he straightened up from his task to leave, and he flashed her a smile that was a bit too familiar. She was about to return the smile in spite of herself when the serving woman entered, carrying a silver tray covered in a crisp linen. The young man left the room with the eyes of the serving maid on his back.

The serving maid turned back to Brigid and smiled, pulling back the linen with a flick of her wrist. The smell of roast mutton and potatoes wafted over to Brigid, reminding her how long ago her last meal was. Brigid cleared away two short stacks of books sitting on the nearest chair and sat down as the maid placed the tray before her. There was a plate heaped with thick cuts of lamb with just a hint of pink remaining and a large potato with crispy skin. Half a loaf of fresh bread lay next to the plate, and an empty goblet sat near a small pitcher holding dark wine. Brigid thanked the serving maid who smiled and left the room.

Considering the amount of food, Brigid was surprised how quickly she cleaned the tray. The wine was warm and spiced nicely, but she allowed herself only a single goblet full. While sorting through the books earlier, she found one detailing the history of Barwick, including the construction of the Viridian Keep. She pulled the book closer to herself and opened to the chapter on the castle.

Brigid was on the last page of the chapter when she heard a small *thunk* from across the room, followed almost immediately by another. She looked up to find an arrow had pierced the spine of a thick book and another arrow protruding from the wall next to the bookcase. The arrow stuck in the spine of the book had pristine white feathers while the feathers of the other arrow were mottled brown. She stared at the arrows for a moment, trying to comprehend why they were there and rose out of her chair. A man then walked through the door, looking over his shoulder and laughing.

He turned and gave a start at seeing Brigid at the table. His hair was long and white, tied in a braid hanging down his back, and, at first, Brigid thought he was well on his way into old age, but when she looked at his unlined face, she could not place his age. His skin was smooth and free of wrinkles, but his light blue eyes had a depth to them that spoke of long years. He wore a white shirt over black pants and highly polished boots. "Pardon my intrusion, madam. Just a bar wager I've won." His words slurred slightly and, when he walked over to the embedded arrows, his walk was the overly cautious meander that those in their cups often adopt. He pulled the arrow out of the wall in one try but could not extract the one buried in the book. He grasped the arrow around the shaft and let the book's pages flop about in his attempt to dislodge the book.

"Stop that!" Brigid crossed the room and picked the book up with both hands. She tried to pull the arrow out of the man's grasp, but his calloused fingers held tightly to the arrow.

"What are you doing?" he asked.

"Stopping you from damaging this book any more than you already have!"

"It's just a book," the man said. "There must be thousands more like it!"

"That's not the point." She gave an extra hard pull, and the book came away in her hands, leaving a gaping hole in the spine. "Look what you've done! Why are you shooting arrows inside a crowded inn?"

"It was a bet, which I won I might add. The other fellow's arrow missed completely." The man held the arrow point close to his eyes and examined it. "Why do you care about some book, anyway? Are you a librarian? Youngest one I've ever seen."

"Yes, I am a librarian, and it's my job to look out for books and keep them safe from drunken idiots!"

The man looked up from the arrow, his eyes intense. The slur vanished and he stood up straight. "I'm hardly drunk. Merely an act to raise the stakes. I am Airl the Archer, known across Irillia as the Greatest Shot Who Ever Lived!" He bowed his head as if expecting applause to burst out from all sides.

"Oh yes, what an achievement for you! If I see you shoot an arrow anywhere near a book again, I'll break it into so many pieces, it'll only be good for picking teeth!" Brigid flounced back to her table, placing the damaged book carefully aside.

"I'd like to see you break one of my arrows," Airl waved the one in his hand. "By the way, I've won more archery contests than there are books in this library."

"I'm sure those awards look great collecting dust on your mantle." Brigid closed the book on the history of Barwick and began re-shelving the books.

"Some of those awards are plaques. They don't sit on the mantle," Airl said and gave Brigid a mocking bow. "Please forgive me for interfering with your work, Madam Librarian." He left the room, narrowly avoiding the door jamb as he went, the careful walk and slight slouch back in place before he crossed the threshold.

Brigid let her anger simmer down as she continued shelving books. When she finished, she almost took the damaged book back to her room to try to repair it before remembering she had nothing to repair it with. She set the book down on the mantelpiece with the spine facing outward, set all her dishes on the tray and went up to her room, ignoring the laughter and chatter coming from the common room.

While she prepared for bed, Brigid decided to leave the inn early in the morning so she could put as much time in as possible on the road north. She slipped between the blankets, and sleep came quickly.

Chapter Five

Icilius ran.

The journey was a short one; less than ten miles lay between Darrow's Well, the small village the forces of the Unbroken Church stopped at for the night, and the isolated   farm Regent Loric sent him to. Icilius still avoided using his Blessing as much as possible, despite how easy and glorifying it felt to be able to do things no mortal man could, but there was no horse to spare. The Regent insisted he arrive with all haste, so Icilius ran slightly faster than a galloping steed. His specially made iron-shod boots barely made contact with the unmarked dirt road as his Blessing fed a steady stream of strength to his legs, coursing like sickly-sweet fire through his veins and leaving the barest tang of copper on his tongue.

The sun was a bare fingernail above the horizon as he ran through sparse pine woods, the road cutting razor straight down the middle of the forest, so his enhanced vision would see any obstruction in his path long before he came upon it. Icilius had a few moments to reflect on the situation before him and prepare himself for a possibly volatile situation. All he knew was Issak, a fellow Paladin, several years his senior, had been on a scouting patrol with a group of Clerics when they'd come across a farm harboring at least two Azorean blasphemers.

Icilius was certain Issak had not requested any aid, as there was not a Paladin Icilius was acquainted with who was as proud or self-assured as Issak, but the Regent sent Icilius to the farm to be sure the situation was under control. The older Paladin would not look kindly upon a newly bled Paladin checking up on him, but orders were to be obeyed, not second-guessed.

The Cage, an enormous iron box on wheels, serving as a means to transport Azoreans to the justice of the Citadel, was dispatched after Icilius. Even though the pilgrimage had left the Citadel less than a week prior, the Cage already held six Azoreans, including one with the profane Talent of freezing water solid at a touch.

Icilius peered down the length of the road and saw the trees begin to thin. The road opened up into a wide channel edged on one side by a fence of split logs, so he began to slow his speed reducing the flow of limitless strength to a bare trickle until he entered the farm property, running at his normal rate.

A large two-story farmstead of unpainted wood sat away from the dirt channel near the treeline, the front door tilting drunkenly open on one hinge. Icilius saw several Clerics huddled not far from the gaping doorway of the barn on the other side of the channel, speaking in low, speculative voices and passing around a flask of forbidden spirits he would overlook for the moment.

Before he reached them, Icilius completely shut off the flow of power from his Blessing, feeling as ever a profound sense of loss as the limits of his natural born flesh settled over him like a tattered old cloak he could not be rid of. He'd heard some Paladins kept a tiny connection to their Blessing open at all times, so the thinnest thread of strength flowed through them, keeping the sense of loss and crushing normalcy at bay. This practice had long ago been denounced by the Church as blasphemous, a blatant waste of the gift bestowed by the Eternal himself. Of course, there was no way to enforce this, but Icilius was stringently compliant.

As he drew abreast of the group of Clerics, he saw another Cleric lying face down on the ground, only a yard or so from the open barn door, unmoving and apparently forgotten by his fellows. Not pausing to consider why the fallen man had been given a wide berth, Icilius moved to kneel down beside the prostrate figure but stopped at a shouted warning from one of the clustered Clerics.

Icilius turned to regard them from where he stood, noting that the flask had vanished as neatly as any street gleeman could have managed. All five Clerics saluted as one, right fist to heart. The man who shouted the warning, near middle age and missing the smallest finger on his right hand, took a step away from his comrades and said, "Apologies, Paladin. You didn't know—no one is to touch that man. He was killed by a foul Azorean Talent. Could be catching."

Icilius nodded. "Report, Cleric."

"Yes, sir," the man said and paused to lick his lips. "Sir, Paladin Issak is questioning the family inside. There is an Azorean whelp who touched Norad there," he jerked his head at the still form of the Cleric, "and Norad's eyes rolled up into his head, and he fell down dead as a beached fish. Nastiest Talent I've ever seen."

Icilius nodded curtly and stepped into the barn, cool and dark despite the rising sun. The inside of the barn smelled strongly of hay and manure with a slight undercurrent of spilled blood that made his stomach twinge uncomfortably. Several stalls lined both sides of the barn, some with horses watching him with a nervous liquid eye.

The stall closest to the door held a woman wearing a tattered cotton dress, kneeling on the hay-strewn ground and holding two small children to her side, their heads buried in her skirts as they softly wept. An older boy, perhaps ten years old, stood behind her, a grubby hand on her shoulder and a twisted, sullen frown for Icilius which he feigned not to see.

A Cleric stood at the mouth of the stall, a standard issue crossbow in the crook of his arm. He saluted Icilius who gave a brief nod in acknowledgment and walked deeper into the barn, where an Azorean man, only a few years older than Icilius himself, stood with his back to an upright post, wrists tied and holding him in place. His face was a mass of bruises and small cuts, so much so Icilius did not see his Azorean markings at first glance. His nose canted off at an awkward angle, leaking a steady stream of blood onto a dirty, torn shirt. He squinted blearily at Icilius through one good eye, the other swollen shut.

Issak stood a pace or two away, wiping bloody hands on a long piece of white linen steadily turning crimson. He'd removed his white coat and hung it over a nearby horse hitch, and his white shirt, unlaced at the neck, was speckled with drops of red like pox. He still wore a hatchet holstered beneath each arm. "Ah, Icilius." Issak said, his voice light and conversational. "I was just finishing here. This filth was living with this good woman and her children, like as not against their will."

"He's my father." The voice came from the older boy in the stall. He glared with unmasked hatred over the side of the stall at Issak. The Cleric keeping watch over the family shot a glare at the boy but said nothing.

"He stopped being your father, boy, when those gray patches came out. The Eternal marked him as one of the damned, but he was too selfish to spare your mother all this trouble," Issak said patiently, still wiping off his hands. "He should've left and taken your blaspheming sister with him. As he didn't, our innocent Cleric Norad paid the price of his decision."

Icilius glanced back at the children in the stall, all of whom were boys. Unease slid like a shadow into his middle. "Where is the daughter?" He asked the older Paladin, who just finished wiping off his hands, now clean save for several scrapes on his knuckles. He slowly made a fist of that hand, watching fresh blood well up from the cuts and slowly run down his clenched fingers.

"Pain is an interesting thing, Icilius; with the Eternal's Blessing, we often forget that as we heal before we can even feel it. I'm only feeling it now because I'd have taken that filth's head clean off at the first strike if I'd been drawing upon the Blessing. I wanted him conscious to feel every hit and remember the pain he caused Norad's family all because of selfishness." Issak watched as his cuts healed over with fresh pink skin in the space of a moment, and Icilius knew he must be drawing upon his Blessing once more.

Icilius approved of the conviction of punishment for the sins of Azoreans but not the punishment itself being carried out by Paladins, though it was not expressly forbidden by the Church. He had no right to say anything against the older man, but the uneasy feeling in his gut intensified when Issak made no attempt to answer his question.

Icilius asked the question again more forcefully, and Issak merely gestured to a darker corner of the barn that Icilius walked right past without noticing. Now he peered into the shadowed depths, and, at first, all he saw was a vague shape on the floor that looked like a jumble of empty sacks. As his eyes adjusted to the dim light, he saw it was the body of a small girl, sprawled on her back. A jagged wound sliced across her throat like a wide, wet smile.

Unexplainable and terrifying rage boiled through him, and Icilius tore his eyes from the gory sight, barely restraining himself from flying at Issak with a knife in each fist. He stood rooted to the ground, breath heaving in his chest and his throat tight, his sudden reaction shocking him more than the sight of the Azorean child's corpse. Icilius knew to kill a child was an abomination, but as this child was an Azorean, the same social mores did not apply. Did they?

To give himself time to calm, Icilius spoke thickly around the tightness of his throat while struggling to keep emotion from his voice. "What did she do to Norad?"

The Azorean, still hanging limply from his restraints, spoke for the first time in a croak. "She . . . just Changed. She can't control—she'd not harm no one— he just grabbed her arm . . ." The Azorean coughed and spat out a gobbet of blood.

"Precisely why all Azoreans are aberrations to society and must be tightly controlled," Issak said, sliding unhurriedly back into his white coat. "Intent is irrelevant. She killed a member of the Unbroken Church, so I executed her."

Icilius felt a chill at Issak's words, even in the humid warmth of the barn. He knew Issak was technically correct; even the accidental killing of a member of the Church bore the penalty of death; but, even in such a straightforward case, the Church preferred to pass judgment and certainly not in front of the accused's family.

"Even had she not killed a Cleric, there would be no way to transport her back to the Citadel without . . ." Icilius glanced over at the rest of the family, and what he saw pulled his attention away from Issak's lecture. The mother and two younger children had not moved since he last saw them, but the older boy had his arm through one of the spaces between the wooden slats separating their stall from the next one over. He'd wrapped his fingers around the shaft of a pitchfork lying propped against the rear wall of the stall. Its tines were coated in dirt or manure but could still inflict serious injury.

The Cleric standing guard over the family had his back to them, his eyes slightly unfocused, obviously lost in his own thoughts. Icilius hesitated, unsure if he should intervene himself or merely draw the Cleric's attention.

In that heartbeat of indecision, the boy moved, yanked the pitchfork through the opening in the slats and, running forward, slid between the Cleric and the wall. The boy brought the pitchfork up in both hands like a spear and charged for Issak, who was just now turning at the surprised yell from the Cleric.

Icilius seized strength from his Blessing, letting it pour into his limbs, but, even as he took his first step toward the running boy, he knew he wouldn't reach him in time. The boy thrust the dirty tines of the pitchfork at Issak's chest, but the Paladin was no longer there. He pivoted smoothly out of the way, allowing the boy's thrust to carry him past. Issak drew one of his long handled hatchets from beneath his coat and neatly severed the boy's spine, nearly taking his head off.

The boy stumbled forward, limbs loose and gangly, and fell at the battered Azorean's feet, the pitchfork under him, blood flowing steadily from the remains of his neck. The boy's mother screamed and would have fainted if she had not been holding onto the other children.

"Get them out of here!" Issak bellowed at the Cleric, seemingly more annoyed with the mother's hysterical wailing than the attempt on his life.

As the Cleric pulled the mother up roughly by an elbow, Icilius took a hesitant step toward Issak, his mind a jumble of confusion, unsure what to do. The added strength from the Blessing flowed through him, seeking an outlet, and he distractedly released his connection to the Blessing and once more came to a stop, paralyzed by indecision.

Issak turned and delivered a vicious backhand to the Azorean's face, breaking his jaw with a loud *crack* and sending tooth fragments flying. "Is there no end to the pain you will cause these good people, scum?" He hissed, and stepped in close, careful to keep away from the slack, hanging jaw and rivulets of fresh blood. He raised the hatchet, still wet with blood and gristle and wiped the blade on the Azorean's already blood-stained shirt.

Issak re-sheathed his weapon with a flourish, turned and headed for the barn door, heedlessly stepping through a wide puddle of spreading blood from the boy's corpse. He paused at Icilius' side and clapped a hand on his shoulder. He waited until two Clerics came in and were busy untying the Azorean before speaking quietly. "Nasty business; not normally how these things go." Icilius, who was staring at the young boy's corpse, met the older man's calm gaze. "I'd appreciate it if you'd not mention the boy in your official report. He did mean to kill me, but the High Regent frowns on the killing of family members of

Azoreans." Issak clapped him once on the shoulder and strode out of the barn, calling loudly for someone to bring him water.

Icilius sat down on an overturned wooden pail, watching the pair of Clerics bearing the Azorean between them across the pool of dark blood still seeping from the boy's corpse. They did not bother to lift the Azorean very high, so his booted feet dragged along the ground and through the pool of blood, leaving twin trails of crimson gore following after.

Icilius was now alone in the barn, save for the corpses of two children, who'd been living and happy only an hour before. He rubbed his hands through his short hair, wishing he could smooth out his thoughts that felt scraped raw as if they'd been thoroughly scrubbed on a washerwoman's board. The anger and uncertainty he'd felt earlier were gone, replaced by a weariness and sadness that staggered him by its depth, especially as he'd done very little that day other than run and observe.

He'd never expected to feel this way during his service to the Church; this was his first major expedition outside of the Citadel, and he never thought something so base and ugly could happen. Icilius firmly took hold of himself; he could not let this experience rattle him. They had leagues to go before reaching the Middle Realm and the true purpose of the journey.

With a titanic effort of will, he rose to his feet, and, by the time he stood at his full height, he'd ruthlessly crushed those thoughts and feelings under a hillside of resolve and forced himself to look to the day's duties. He took a step toward the barn door, resolutely not looking at either corpse, and after the first step, moving was easier. That was the way of most things; they became easier with repetition.

Chapter Six

When Owin opened his eyes and saw the curved roof over his head, he was momentarily at a loss to recall where he was. By the time he sat up on the mattress, everything came flooding back to him. He braced for an avalanche of self-pity and regret, and, while there was plenty of both, they did not amount to the mountain he'd expected.

He splashed some water on his face, still not used to the feeling of the hardened patches beneath his fingers. He then pulled his boots on and ducked out of the door. He looked up for the sun and had to remind himself, when he couldn't see it, that he stood on the floor of a canyon at least fifty yards deep. It was cool in the shade of the nearby canyon wall. Owin made his way to the Mess, the building Meryl pointed out the day before and claimed food would be waiting for him. It was the closest stone building to his particular cluster of grass-covered mounds.

Inside several long tables sat in rows, reminding him forcibly of that fateful common room not too long ago. The walls of the large room were unadorned, though the stone floor was well swept, and the large fireplace on the opposite side of the room was spotless, save for a small pile of unlit logs in the grate. He joined the end of a short line of Azoreans leading up to a small window cut into the wall through which each received their food. When it was Owin's turn, he received a bowl of porridge and a wooden spoon from a Azorean man wearing a dirty apron on the other side of the window.

Though the benches offered enough seats for some four dozen Azoreans to eat at once, less than a quarter of the seats were occupied. Owin quickly scanned those seated to see if any of them were one of the three people in the entire Colony he knew but was unsurprised to see no one familiar. Owin sat at the table closest to the door and began to shovel food down. He'd always eaten quickly, no matter how many times his mother had lectured him on the importance of eating slowly and the very real possibility of choking to death.

The porridge was filling and hot and, by the time his spoon scraped the bottom of the bowl, he realized he was full. Depositing his bowl and spoon in a bin by the door, Owin walked back outside. He scarcely had time to close the door after himself before words formed in his mind that were not his own. *Good morning, Owin. I see you have just finished your morning meal. Would you be kind enough to meet Ox and myself in the Training Pavilion, the largest building to your left?* Owin paused and looked surreptitiously around to see if he could spot Telas. Words formed once again in his mind. *Unless your Talent is the ability to see through stone walls, you will not be able to find me.* Owin grinned to himself and walked over to the building Telas had indicated.

The structure was the largest he had seen in the Colony, perhaps twice the size of the mess hall. Unlike all the other stone buildings, this one was capped with a domed roof, its highest point some twenty feet above ground. There were no windows on the side that faced Owin as he approached, only a pair of wooden doors. He pulled open the right hand door and walked inside onto a sand-covered floor. The single large room inside was lit by several flickering torches mounted along the walls. Odd constructions of wood and cloth lined the walls, some vaguely man-like in shape but others like nothing he'd seen before.

A long table laden with an assortment of objects sat near the center of the room, and next to the table stood Ox, Telas and a second Azorean woman Owin did not know. She was not as tall as Telas, though she was broader and more heavily muscled. She had long red hair tied back in a braid and a black eye patch over her right eye. As Owin came up to the waiting trio, he saw the flesh around the woman's covered eye was scarred and puckered as if she had lost her eye in a disagreement with something sharp and scalding.

Ox clapped a hand on Owin's shoulder, and Owin felt his knees buckle slightly from the force of the blow. "I see you've laid eyes on Oriana One-Eye, our Mistress of the Battle here in the Colony." The flame-haired woman nodded slightly, her one good eye looking Owin up and down.

"Oriana is in charge of training all new Azoreans and help them on their way to mastering use of their Talent. As I said last night, first we must determine exactly what your Talent is and how much control you have over it." Telas gestured towards the object-strewn table. All the objects were small, the largest being an iron serving platter half covered in rust. There were several cups of various shapes, small rocks, different sized knives, even a battered helmet. "We have here an assortment of things for you to try your Talent on." Telas picked up one of the knives and placed it close to the table's edge away from the other objects.

"Let's try this knife first." She stepped away from the table and motioned for Owin to stand closer to the knife. "It is usually the case when an Azorean's Talent first appears, he or she is under stress or feeling great emotion. Once first used, a Talent becomes much easier to use with concentration." Telas said this briskly, as if she'd repeated it many times.

"I know it may seem as fruitless as trying to catch the wind in your hands, but it may help to envision the time when you first used your Talent. What was going through your mind? Concentrate on that and try to make this knife move."

Owin looked down at the knife and thought back to that night in the common room. The fear. That terrible feeling of everything he thought he knew about himself being ripped away by the yells and jeers of those men. The sudden shifting in his mind and the abrupt, nameless awareness of the approaching cup.

The knife remained impassive, lying where Telas placed it. Owin closed his eyes and thought of the cup suddenly veering away from him, the point in the air where it had changed its flight and the invisible ripple in the air he'd felt from the spot where the cup veered off course.

"Open your eyes, Owin." He opened his eyes at Telas' words and saw the knife still lying on the table. He was about to ask why she told him to open his eyes when he saw the knife was no longer lined up with the edge of the table as it had been a moment before. "Try it again Owin, but this time, keep your eyes open."

Owin turned back to the knife, once again concentrating on that moment in time when the flying cup suddenly changed direction. Owin saw the blade tremble and then slide backwards a few inches on the table. "Very good, Owin." Telas smiled, and Ox slapped him on the back. Owin winced and thought he could almost feel his ribs flex and spring back into shape from the force of the blow.

Telas slid a metal cup to the side of the table where knife had lain. Owin turned his attention to the cup and formed the same image in his mind of the point of impact and, just before the cup began to slide across the table, Owin caught a flash of a colorless nimbus surrounding the cup like hot air wavering above an open flame. He gave the nimbus a mental push, and the cup slid across the table away from him in the direction he indicated in his mind. The cup clattered against the large iron serving tray and came to a stop. Owin formed the colorless nimbus around the cup in his mind and pushed on the nimbus in the opposite direction. He pushed with more force than before, and the cup shot off the end of the table and clattered to the floor.

Telas let the cup lie where it landed and slid one of the rocks to the side of the table. Owin formed the nimbus around the rock in his mind and pushed on it, but nothing happened. His sudden elation at what he could do faded, and the nimbus around the rock wavered just as his concentration winked out. He forced himself to concentrate on the stone and tried to move it again. Still nothing.

"Something is wrong. It's not working." Owin looked up at Telas, who stared back at him for a moment before saying, "try the cup again."

Owin looked down at the cup, pictured the nimbus around it in his mind and pushed. The cup rolled obediently under the table. Owin looked back at Telas, who was pressing a finger to her lips in thought, eyes on the unmovable stone. She smiled suddenly and said, "I believe I have the answer. Your Talent allows you to move only metal objects with your mind. Are you familiar with how a lode stone works?"

"Yes, it attracts iron filings." Owin had seen one demonstrated in school.

"It seems your Talent works in a similar manner. By either attracting or repelling metal or iron, you can move the object where you wish using your mind."

"'Tis always exciting when an Azorean first discovers what his Talent can do!" Ox grinned broadly.

Telas glanced at Ox and then at Oriana, who had silently watched Owin's first display of his Talent with her arms crossed over her chest and a blank expression on her face. She didn't look bored, exactly, but as if Owin's first display of Talent was nothing of real importance.

"Ox and I have some business to be about, so we will leave you in Oriana's capable hands." Telas placed her hands on Ox's arm and firmly steered him toward the door. Ox let her, but it was plain he was reluctant to leave for some reason. "You will receive your weekly schedule tomorrow, Owin," Telas called over her shoulder as she pulled Ox through the open door.

Owin watched them leave and turned back to where Oriana was standing, just in time to catch a glimpse of her fist filling his vision. The next thing he knew, he was lying on his back on the sand, feeling a trickle of something warm slowly leak from his nose, pooling on his upper lip.

Owin looked up at Oriana standing over him with arms crossed over her chest and a sneer on her face. Owin had certainly been in a fight or two in his life but had never been hit with such reckless disdain. He stumbled to his feet, the room wobbling slightly. "I'm done. You and every other Azorean can piss off." He headed for the door, smearing his hand across his nose and wiping it on his shirt without looking at the blood. He half expected to feel a hand on his shoulder or hear her call him back, but neither happened.

He slammed open the door and stalked outside to find Ox and Telas standing and watching him as if they were waiting for him. "Owin, lad—" Ox began, but Owin kept walking.

Owin. The voice in his head was soft but insistent.

Owin spun on his heel and flashed a rude gesture at the pair of Azoreans. "Stay out of my head!"

It is understandable how you're feeling, but you have no other place to go, the voice in his head replied, just as softly.

"I'm not staying here to get knocked around by some tavern thug!"

Oriana appeared at the door of the Pavilion. "You are a soft spoiled village boy. Our life is not easy. You need—"

"Enough, Oriana," Ox said and took a step towards Owin. "Lad, I had much the same reaction when I—"

"You're eight feet tall and wide as a door. You can't think I'd believe—" Owin threw up his hands. "No. I'm done." He looked about at both canyon walls, searching for the staircase back up. He spotted the entrance to the staircase some hundred yards or so away, past some wood and stone buildings and took off in that direction.

He passed several Azoreans in the midst of various tasks; some of them looked up as he passed and offered smiles in greeting, but Owin ignored them. He heard a female voice calling his name, but he ignored it as well, assuming it must be Telas. Owin almost reached the first step of the monolithic staircase when someone grabbed the tail of his shirt from behind. He whirled around, ready to punch whoever it was square in the mouth. It was Meryl.

"What?" His voice was harsher than he meant it to be, but at the moment he didn't care. "Did Telas send you after me?"

Meryl frowned. "No. Even without my enhanced hearing, I could have heard you shouting on the other side of the Colony. Where are you going?"

"Out of this pit. After that, I'm not sure, but it has to be better than here."

"Because Oriana punched you?" Meryl asked, glancing down at the blood on his sleeve.

"Not just because of that. This is . . ." Owin cast about for a suitable description. "Not fair." He sat down on the first stair, running both hands through his hair.

"No, it's not fair." Meryl sat down next to him, though there was hardly enough room on the step. "My life before my Change was not perfect, but I'd go back to it on hands and knees if I could remove these patches and climb out of here."

"What was your life like before?" Owin asked.

Meryl glanced at him for a moment, as if in consideration. She pulled a leather thong from beneath the neck of her dress and absently fingered the battered thimble that it ran through. "I was— am a cobbler's daughter from Vera Pelle, not far from the Drannon. I was about to be apprenticed to a seamstress when the Change happened. My parents tried to hide me for a few days, but one night I overheard my father trying to convince my mother it would be kinder to smother me in my sleep. I left home that night and haven't looked back."

"That's— awful." Owin was stunned. He tried to picture how his parents would react if he had gone back to Vridian Ford after the Change. His father was Mayor; surely he could have made the townspeople understand, in time, their preconceived notions about Azoreans were wrong.

"Yes, it is awful. Every Azorean that has undergone the Change believes their life is over, and it is, to a certain extent. Then they come to the Colony, and they discover a new life. I don't even think about my old life anymore." Only the slight waver in her voice told Owin this wasn't exactly true. She caught him looking at the thimble and she tucked it back beneath her dress.

"My father is the Mayor of my village. Maybe—he could keep me hidden until everyone could be convinced I wasn't a threat."

Meryl shook her head sadly. "The daughter of the King of the Northern Realm went through the Change a year before I did. He managed to keep it a secret for a few days until word got out of the castle, and there was nearly a city-wide riot when the King refused to send her away. All of his servants quit, and he still wouldn't budge. Some noble hired an assassin from the Thieves' Guild, and they crept into the castle one night and slit her throat."

"So . . . I guess I really don't have anywhere to go." Owin felt like a trap door had opened suddenly in his middle, and he turned his head away from Meryl so she wouldn't see his eyes fill with tears.

"No, you're stuck with us." Owin could hear the smile in Meryl's voice even though he still couldn't look at her. He felt her hand on his arm. "Oriana is rough but not more than she has to be. I still have a couple scars on my knuckles from where they hit her teeth."

"You fought her too?" Owin hadn't considered the Colony would make women go through that as well.

"Of course. It's thanks to Oriana I've been able to protect myself more than once when I've been out in Irillia."

Owin looked down at the dried blood on his sleeve. "I suppose I expected her to hold back a little."

"She doesn't because she knows no one on Irillia will be holding back if they have a mind to hurt you. What Oriana teaches you now could save your life one day, or another Azorean's."

Owin finally could meet her eyes safely and even smile slightly. "Well, I suppose I will stay, for a little while."

Meryl smiled back, and they both rose to their feet. "I've heard before Oriana came to the Colony, Ox was the combat trainer. Even without using his Talent, I'm sure he hits much harder."

Once he made his way back into the training building and stood in front of Oriana One-Eye, he asked, already knowing the answer but wanting to hear it from her, "Why did you hit me?"

"To see how you would react. You can tell much about a person in how they take a punch. Everyone could do with learning how to take a punch properly, especially you." Oriana grinned at him, her one good eye steady on his face. "Now you're going to see me coming. Let's see what you can do." Her left fist was moving towards his head before the last word was out of her mouth. Owin tried to knock it aside with his arm as he'd seen other men do in common room brawls. He managed to move her fist aside enough so it only clipped his right ear, but, before he could even register the pain, her other fist found his left eye, and he went down again.

Owin could feel his eye begin to swell and waited until the bright flashes of light stopped exploding in his head before even attempting to climb to his feet. Oriana grinned even wider, the edges of the scars radiating from beneath her eye patch turning white. "Are you one of those people who just like hitting other people?" Owin asked, gingerly touching his swollen eye.

"It is one of my favorite parts about training new Azoreans," Oriana admitted. "Get up. Let me see you try to hit me."

After climbing back to his feet, Owin threw the hardest punch he could with most of his weight behind it. Oriana dodged beneath it with unhurried ease and hit him in the side with two quick blows which somehow hurt worse than getting hit in the face and drove all the breath out of his body.

Owin lay curled on the ground, eyes scrunched shut. Oriana paced back and forth in front of him but didn't say anything. Owin remained where he was, simply concentrating on one breath at a time. Breathing in hurt much more than out, but after several deep breaths, the pain began to lessen. After what must have been a quarter of an hour, Owin uncurled and slowly sat up. Oriana stood over him, looking down at him with an unreadable expression. Owin thought she was about to command him to get to his feet again, but instead she launched into a lecture about basic defense and the proper way to hit someone without hurting yourself in the process. It sounded like Oriana had delivered this lecture many times before, and Owin supposed she had if she were in charge of training all new Azoreans.

When Owin's stomach began to tell him it was past time for the midday meal, he interrupted her lecture about the benefits of using your feet as well as your hands in combat. Oriana stared at him with her one good eye for a moment and then commented one missed meal would hardly do him any harm and continued on with her lecture as if he had not spoken.

In the afternoon, she set him on a long and complicated routine of building up his strength, aided by the constructions of wood and cloth he had noted early in the morning. She also informed him he would start running laps around the entire colony every morning before first meal, and she would watch to make sure it was done. Oriana finally dismissed him for the day, saying he had just a quarter of an hour to get to the dining hall before it closed for the night.

Owin stumbled outside to find dusk well underway and ran to the dining hall, his way illuminated by flickering torches in iron sconces spread out every few yards. He was very conscious of aching muscles all over his body and sweat soaking through his tunic, though the cool night air felt good on his slick skin.

Once inside the dining hall, he saw only a few Azoreans scattered about the room, but he was so hungry he ate whatever the Azorean behind the counter handed him so fast he barely tasted it. He stumbled through the darkened colony and was scarcely able to find his own dome before sleep took him.

The next morning Owin woke to nearly every muscle in his body tight and sore, his face still feeling like a bowl of bread dough just kneaded by half the women in Vridian Ford. He hadn't had time to change out of his sweaty clothes before sleep took him the night before and was surprised to find a neat pile of folded clothes just inside his door. It was only a simple tunic and pants of a pale green, but he peeled off his old clothes and shrugged on his new ones gratefully.

Owin ducked out of his hut and headed towards the dining hall before he remembered what Oriana had commanded him to do the previous day. He considered eating first and running after, but Oriana had warned him she would be watching, and he really had no interest in giving her any excuse to hit him again. So he took off at a brisk run around his section of the low huts, staying close to the canyon wall.

Completing an entire loop around the Colony took longer than Owin thought, though he continued running until he had completed two laps around. As he headed for the dining hall for the second time that morning, he reflected while he was completely out of breath and sweating, at least the running had eased away some of the tightness from his muscles.

The dining hall was much more crowded than the previous night; nearly all the tables were packed elbow to elbow. Owin accepted a bowl of corn mush with raisins from the

Azorean behind the counter and sat down at one of the few empty seats. Owin's spoon rose and fell without his taking much notice of what he was eating. He had never seen so many Azoreans in one place before. No one Azorean had exactly the same pattern of gray patches on their skin, and there seemed to even be a wide variation in how many gray patches each Azorean possessed.

Owin scanned the seated Azoreans to see if he could find Meryl but was not surprised when he didn't see her. An older Azorean man came along Owin's table and stopped next to him. "Hello Owin; my name is Beor, Second Quartermaster, and Ox has tasked me with making up your schedule for this week." The man's head was completely bald, though the crown of his head was covered with so many gray patches it looked almost like he wore a gray cap. He held out a small scroll of paper tied with a bit of string.

"Schedule?" Owin asked. He took the offered paper after a moment's hesitation.

If Beor noticed Owin's hesitation at all, he gave no sign. "Yes. In order for our Colony to function, each member must contribute by sharing the work. We can hardly hire outside servants, and this way, each member of the Colony can take pride in contributing to the continued existence of their home." He gestured to the paper in Owin's hand. "Your schedule tells you where to be and at what time each day. Everyone must do their part." Beor gave a slight nod and walked away.

Owin unrolled the paper and found a small list for every day of the week, written in a precise hand. He had tasks assigned for every day of the week, as well as training with Oriana for a few hours every other day. He understood the need for practice, though he certainly wasn't looking forward to her idea of 'training.'

As he looked closer at the tasks he was assigned for later that day, he heard a familiar voice say his name from across the table. He looked up to see Meryl seated across from him, a slight smile on her lips. She wore a plain blue dress today, one with short sleeves showing off slender arms. Owin grinned back, genuinely pleased to see a familiar face. "How was your first night after training?"

"I don't remember much of it; I was dead asleep."

"How's the face? Doesn't seem to be much swelling."

"Still sore. Guess I should be thankful she didn't leave any lasting damage."

Meryl grimaced for a moment, moving her tongue over one of her front teeth. "She hit me hard enough to knock one of my teeth out. Theryn was able to put it back good as new. He's one of the Colony's healers."

Owin felt a twinge of annoyance at this; he certainly would have liked a healer to look him over after his session with Oriana. He opened his mouth to ask where he could find this Theryn when an Azorean man stopped in the aisle behind Meryl, studying Owin with a practiced eye.

He was about Owin's age with the olive skin and almond-shaped eyes common to natives of the Drannon Desert. He had black hair cut very close to his skull and high cheekbones, making his face very angular. The only visible gray patch on his face was a line of gray slashed down over his left eye, as if put there by the cutting stroke of a knife. He leaned over the table, over Meryl's head as if she wasn't there, and extended his hand. "You must be the latest addition to the Colony. I'm Zaul."

Owin shook the offered hand without thinking and gave his name. He glanced at Meryl who was bent over the table, since Zaul was still leaning over her. Meryl did not meet his eyes but stared at the scuffed wood of the tabletop, her face expressionless.

Zaul looked down at Meryl as if seeing her for the first time. "Ah, Meryl, isn't it? Don't you have some tasks you should be getting to? If not, I'm sure the Quarter will be interested to know you have so much free time."

Meryl nodded silently, her chin almost scraping the tabletop. She slid out from under Zaul's body and walked away down the aisle, not looking back. Owin felt an instant dislike for Zaul as he sat down in Meryl's abandoned seat. "We were in the middle—"

Zaul continued as if Owin hadn't spoken. "I hear Ox speaks highly of your Talent. Says you'll make a fine Soldier."

"A Soldier?"

"We must always be prepared. Everyone on Irillia hates us, none more so than the Unbroken Church. Why, they hired some mercenaries to attack us in the middle of the night not two months ago." Zaul leaned towards Owin, his tone becoming conspiratorial. "As a Soldier of the Colony, you needn't socialize with commoners like Meryl. You'll soon discover the pecking order around here, and as you'll be a Soldier, you can take pride in being at the top."

"No thanks." Owin rose to his feet and walked out of the mess, leaving his half-finished porridge behind. He suspected he had just made life more difficult for himself in the Colony, but he didn't care. As the mayor's son, he had met a few wealthy merchants passing through Vridian Ford and had seen them act in a similar fashion towards the other townspeople and wanted nothing to do with someone who felt his status elevated him above others.

Once outside, he paused to check his schedule. A deep bell sounded from a tower at the end of the Colony opposite most of the sleeping mounds, and a steady stream of Azoreans soon came out of the Mess, finishing dozens of conversations as they all moved off in separate directions for their morning's tasks.

Owin's first task was a training session with Telas. He spent three hours with her in the Pavilion, moving various metal objects in different directions and speeds across the table. As he worked at his task, he caught glimpses of other Azoreans training in other parts of the large tent. A trio of women shot arrows from longbows at the very back, aiming at round shields mounted to posts of varying heights. A pair of Azorean men, stripped to the waist, cut away at each other with blunted swords.

When the three bells sounded for the midday meal, Telas commented on his   progress, though she thought he might have made even more if he had spent less time gawking at the other Azoreans like a village boy during his first time in a big city brothel. As Owin walked to the mess, he reflected how his schoolteacher had said something similar, though less colorfully, to his father; it had been the prettier girls in the class he had been staring at then.

After a meal of thin barley soup and thick slices of bread, he carried buckets of water from the stream to dump in large steaming cauldrons filled with dirty laundry, tended by several older women Azoreans expertly wielding long, flat-bladed wooden paddles. Then he brought more buckets of water from the same stream to water the expansive crop patches on the other side of the Colony. As Owin's family did not farm, he had only a basic understanding of growing crops but was impressed with the orderly rows of corn, wheat and potatoes.

For his last task of the day, he reported to the smithy, housed under a large canvas tent not far from the thin tower that held the Colony's messenger ravens. The tent was supported on thick iron poles and looked to be scorched by fire in several places. Before he even set foot inside, he could feel the heat from the forge and now knew the source of the hammering he heard earlier in the day.

There was only one Azorean in the smithy: a man with wide shoulders and thick arms, and, while he stood near a rack that held hammers of all sizes and shapes, he was sitting on the anvil itself, smoking a large pipe with a bowl that looked able to hold an entire cup of tea. He looked to be past middle age with thinning brown hair and a thick mustache and eyebrows. He wore a stained leather apron over a chest completely bare of hair, though criss-crossed with pale scars and pants cut off at the knee.

Owin stood in the entryway of the tent for a moment in silence, staring at the man who studied him over the glowing bowl of his pipe. The hand that held the pipe only had three fingers with scarred flesh stretched tight where the other two should be. He pulled himself off the anvil with a grunt and walked closer to Owin, pipe in one hand and smoke streaming out of his nose like a dragon in one of the stories he'd been told as a child. "So, you're the latest that idiot quartermaster has decided to try with me."

Owin hesitated, not sure how to answer, but the man kept talking as if not expecting a response. "Haven't seen you before, so he must be scraping the bottom of the barrel."

"I'm new to the Colony; my name—"

"Didn't ask for it. Let's see what you can do with the bellows before I need to know your name." The man clamped his yellowed teeth around the stem of the pipe and lead Owin over to the low forge filled with glimmering coals and a small flame burning in the center. He showed Owin how to work the bellows and described exactly how hot the fire needed to be, speaking of subtle shades of color Owin had never heard of before. Heph had Owin demonstrate on the bellows three times in a row before he grunted in approval and got to work on forging new ax heads without further comment.

Owin watched him with interest and worked the bellows every time the man gave him a nod. The flame threw up sparks every time he pushed down on the bellows, but fortunately, the forge itself stood between Owin and the flying sparks. More than once a spark would alight on the man's leather apron and sit there, twinkling away like a star until it burned itself out.

The blacksmith continued his work for another half hour before he set down his hammer and tongs and wiped the sweat dripping from his face with a long, dirty piece of cloth that hung from an iron loop in the ceiling near the forge. He turned to look at Owin still standing ready by the bellows, removed his pipe still clenched in his teeth despite having been finished, and said, "Best take a break. Don't need you fainting on the job."

Owin blinked as sweat ran into his eye and wiped his own sweating brow on his sleeve, noticing for the first time how warm he felt standing so close to the forge; the rhythm of the clanging hammer had been hypnotic, and he'd been enthralled watching the blacksmith work.

The blacksmith cleaned the dottle out of his pipe with a long fingernail and refilled it from a bulging leather purse he wore on a belt under his leather apron. "Now I know you can work the bellows, what is your name?"

"Owin. I'm new to the Colony."

"Explains why I haven't seen you before. Name is Heph." He lit his pipe from a thin piece of wood kindled at the forge. "Some call me Three Fingered Heph." He studied Owin as he pulled several times on his pipe to get it started, as if waiting for him to react.

Not knowing what else to say, Owin said, "Doesn't really fit you. You have seven fingers, not three." He wiped his face again and moved a little closer to the cooler air coming from the tent's entrance.

Heph grinned as he puffed out smoke. "Very true. Don't care for the name but can't change it now. Folk at least know enough not to say it to my face." He studied Owin in silence for a few moments, steadily smoking away, and said, "Heard you can move metal and iron without touching it."

"Yes, not very well yet."

"Can't imagine why the Quarter didn't try you here sooner. Your Talent would make the choice obvious."

"I liked watching you work. We had a blacksmith in my village, but I didn't spend much time there."

"Too busy chasing women?"

"What? No, I—" Owin saw Heph was grinning at him and didn't finish his denial.

"Colony is the worst place on Irillia for gossip. Even I hear it, and I avoid most folk. Must have a lot of free time, being son of the mayor."

"Yeah, you could say that."

"Just did. Met a lot of your type before I Changed, and you're all from the same mold, though you seem to have learned not to look down your nose at everyone."

Owin was unsure what to say to this, so he remained silent.

"Meant no offense. Just those as are better off than others seem to have a high opinion of themselves."

Owin nodded. "My father's the mayor, but we were not any richer than anyone else. He was elected two years ago, and he'll have to run for election again next year." He felt a twinge of remorse as he thought of his family, slightly weaker than the day before.

Heph merely gave a grunt of acknowledgment at this and turned back to the crackling forge. "Still have lots of work. Never enough bloody hours in the day."

Owin moved back to man the bellows and lost himself once more in watching Heph work until the dinner bell sounded, though he barely heard it over the steady clang of the hammer. Heph lifted his pipe in farewell but continued on his work, and Owin made his way out of the tent, wiping his face on his sweat-soaked tunic and grateful for the slight breeze on his hot skin.

At the evening meal of mutton and squash, Owin looked for Meryl but did not see her. He gave a wide berth to Zaul, who seemed to be in the midst of an animated conversation with half the Azoreans at his table. After the meal, an older Azorean man with long black hair tinged with gray stood on a tabletop and began to declaim 'The Tale of Horvald Hogsnatch' in a deep, carrying voice. Owin heard the story before and only listened for a few minutes before quietly leaving the Mess and making his way to his dome, where he fell asleep shortly after his head hit the pillow.

Chapter Seven

Brigid woke to a light tapping sound coming from the door leading out to the hallway. She certainly wasn't expecting anyone, so she tried to ignore it. The tapping continued for several moments with slight pauses at random. Brigid pulled her pillow over her head, but the pillow was thin and didn't do much to muffle the sound.

She finally swung her legs over the side of the bed and stood up, thinking perhaps it was Master Pynce with some urgent news from home. She cast about the room for something to throw over her nightgown but then realized she was still wearing her dress from the day before. She paused at the door with her hand on the knob for a moment then pulled it open a crack, wedging the side of her foot against the edge of the door, just in case it was not the innkeeper.

The person in the hall was both the last person she expected or wanted to see in the middle of the night. Airl stood there with a large quiver peeking over his shoulder and carrying his strung bow, casting furtive glances down the hall. When he saw Brigid staring back at him through the cracked door, he said, "Certainly took your time answering! No one else would."

Before she could open her mouth to reply, he shouldered his way into the room, nearly bowling Brigid over as he pushed her aside and closed the door softly behind him. "What in the Eternal's beard do you think you're doing?" Brigid demanded, inwardly cringing at how high pitched her voice sounded.

"Nearly losing my hearing, at the moment," Airl said quietly, and from the little light coming through her window, Brigid saw him set his weight against the door. Her first thought was that the man was still drunk, feigned or not, but when he met her gaze, his eyes were steady and focused. "I'm trying to avoid being caught in a tight spot, so I'm calling upon that fabled small town hospitality."

"That fabled hospitality does not extend to being woken in the dead of night," Brigid said, folding her arms.

"Believe me, I like this no more than you do," Airl said. "I lost a wager earlier tonight, and the amount was for more coin than I have in my purse, so I wrote a Bill of Debt, which was accepted, but then, apparently, was sold to the Thieves' Guild who came to collect."

Brigid resisted asking about the Guild, as she knew it would make her seem naive, and she had enough condescension on that subject already. "You mean Irillia's best archer lost an archery contest? Did you tell them about your numerous awards?"

"If it'd been an archery contest, I wouldn't be standing here now," Airl said. "It was at cards which I have no great skill at." He fell silent, placing a finger unnecessarily against his lips. A floorboard creaked just outside Brigid's door, and the door latch rattled.

Airl listened and whispered, "He's moved on." He looked about the darkened room and pointed to the rumpled bedclothes. "We haven't much time. Tie some of the sheets together so we can go out the window."

"What do you mean, 'We?' I'm not going anywhere. You said the Guild just wants you."

"They'll want you too when they find you helped hide me from them."

"I did nothing like that! You barged into my—"

Airl held up a hand. "Can you protest and tie at the same time?"

"No, you can break your fool neck jumping out the window," Brigid said coldly.

Airl left the door and tore the bedclothes off the straw mattress as fast as any maid and began knotting two together.

"That won't work. Do you honestly think it will hold two people?"

"I've tried it myself, and it will work, especially as it's one floor." Airl cinched the knot tight. "Pack up your things unless you want them sold on the street in the morning."

Brigid muttered several curses under her breath and hurriedly stuffed her few belongings pell-mell into the saddlebags.

Airl tied a third sheet to the end of the makeshift rope and secured its end to the bedpost. He moved to the small window, opened it and threw the other end of the rope out into the night. A loud crash rattled the door in the frame causing Brigid to flinch and nearly drop the purse she was tying to her belt.

Airl picked up his bow and pulled an arrow out of his quiver. Something struck the door again, and the latch snapped. A man wearing bits of leather armor over a filthy black shirt stood in the doorway and caught the door as it rebounded off the wall. "'Ere you are, archer! Taken to hiding behind skirts, 'ave we?" He turned his head to bellow over his shoulder, and an arrow streaked into his right cheek and punched through his left with a shower of blood and bits of tooth. The force whipped his head around sharply, and he fell to his knees, hands pressed to the tattered ruins of his mouth.

"Go. Now." Airl said, his calm voice at odds with the sudden violence. Brigid stared at the man moaning in agony on the floor and at the flecks of blood dotting the door and wall like freckles.

Airl grabbed her wrist and pulled her over to the window, and, by the time she stood in front of it, she managed to shove down her horror and take hold of herself. Brigid maneuvered her way up onto the narrow sill, sitting with her legs dangling out into empty air. Goose flesh erupted over her exposed skin, though she was more worried about climbing down the side of a building in a dress and a brisk breeze stirring up at the wrong moment.

Brigid lowered herself through the window, and it wasn't until she was hanging her full weight from the makeshift rope did she wonder if the knots would hold. The knots did their job, and she lowered herself a few feet until her arms began to ache from supporting all her weight, so she let go, after reminding herself she was only on the second floor. In the brief moment when she fell freely through the air, her middle seemed to leap up into her throat, and the thought of broken bones flashed through her mind. A moment later, her boots struck the cobblestones of the alley behind the inn, and she reached out to touch the side of the building to steady herself.

She looked up just in time to cover her head with both arms as her saddlebags fell limply onto her back before tumbling to the ground. Brigid cursed at the lack of a warning and picked them up before moving a few steps away as Airl's booted feet appeared over the window ledge.

He slid down more elegantly than she had managed, propping his feet against the side of the building and seeming to stroll backwards down the wall. As soon as his boots hit the ground, he took off down the alley without a word, and Brigid hurried after, her saddlebags tucked under one arm.

A shout came from behind them, and, as they turned down another alley, Brigid risked a glance over her shoulder and saw a head poking out of her recently vacated window. The man gave another shout as he spotted Brigid.

Halfway down the next dim street, lit only by flickering lamplight from posts on each corner, Brigid came to a sudden stop when she thought of Mist, still in the *Ledger's* stable. Airl doubled back when he realized she was no longer following.

"My horse. I can't leave her behind," Brigid said.

"We can't go back now," Airl took hold of her upper arm to pull her after him, but she wrenched her arm free.

"I borrowed her from a farm; the family needs her back!"

"I will gladly pay you twice what she's worth if we keep going," Airl said tersely, his eyes on the alley's mouth they had just passed.

Brigid wavered, unable to decide, and Airl tried to pull her again, and this time she let him. Master Pynce was unlikely to let Mist starve, she reasoned, and what she would fetch in the market would cover the rest of her bill.

Airl lead her down three more streets in rapid succession, staying in the shadows when possible. He brought them to a halt before a wide open space ringed with a short stone wall. Trees stood in clusters beyond the wall, and now Brigid caught the faint tinkling of falling water.

Airl squinted into the darkness over the low wall. The nearest source of light came from a lamp several yards away and did very little to part the shadows hanging over the park, as Brigid guessed it must be. "There's someone there," Airl murmured. "Wouldn't have seen him if he hadn't moved. Might only be a beggar but can't take the chance."

Brigid blinked in surprise, wondering how Airl's eyes seemed to pierce the darkness while hers seemed so inadequate. "We'll have to go around." He took off back up the street, and Brigid nearly was at his side when he darted left without warning, between a haberdasher and a butcher's shop. She followed down the narrow space between the shops and emerged in a cobblestoned alley that ran behind the shops.

Airl waited for her to nearly catch up and then took off down the alley. Brigid followed doggedly after, though she kept one eye on the ground in front of her boots for anything that might trip her up. The alley was also much darker than the streets had been, and she expected to fall flat on her face at any moment. Vague shapes loomed out of the darkness as she passed, and she was sure more than one was that of a person, sleeping on the ground.

She glanced up in time to see Airl stop suddenly and thrust out his right arm in her path. Brigid tried to stop, but her chest struck his outstretched arm before she was able. Airl's arm only moved slightly forward, though to Brigid it felt like running headlong into a sturdy fence post.

Even as she rebounded off his arm, something whistled through the air less than a hand's-breadth in front of her face and snapped against the back wall of some unknown shop.

A curse came from down the connecting alley mouth. "That's why I hate bloody crossbows," Airl said, holding his bow in one hand like a stave and drawing one of his long knives with his other. He spun the blade around in his hand until he held it by the end of the grip, near the pommel, the blade pressing flat against the side of his wrist. "Makes every thug fancy himself an archer, no skill involved."

Airl stepped forward a few paces and turned to meet three men who now stood at the mouth of the alley. Two of them were bare chested under dirty vests and the third, who hung back clumsily trying to reload a small battered crossbow, was obviously drunk. "Gentlemen. You have one chance to walk away and keep what few teeth you have left."

The man on the right grinned, showing several gaps in his teeth. "It's gentlemen we'll be when we collect a fat purse for bringing you in." He pulled out a dagger, and the other man, with several scars crossing his face, produced a short club capped in iron.

The man with the club attacked first, feigning with his fist while swinging widely with his club. Airl ignored the feint, blocked the club strike with the flat of his blade and hit him square in the face with a quick punch with the fist holding his bow. The man's nose shattered, spraying blood in a fine mist, and Airl kicked him low in the chest, sending him sprawling to the ground.

The gap-toothed man bent to pick up the fallen club and rushed Airl in a crouch, both weapons held low. The dagger darted at Airl's middle, but a quick flick of one of the ends of his bow knocked the blade from his grasp. Airl calmly stepped back a pace as the man pressed his attack, the club blurring in wild swings that hit nothing but air.

Airl reversed his hold on his knife, and it flashed out to meet his opponent's next swing, taking his hand off at the wrist. The man fell on his side, screaming and trying to contain the fountain spray of blood from the ragged stump. Airl flicked his knife like the handle of a whip, wiped it once against his leg and slid it back into its sheath before turning to contemplate the last man, who was trying in vain to load another bolt.

"That's another thing," Airl said, and Brigid noted he wasn't even breathing hard. "Crossbows take too long to reload, even with practice."

The man finally succeeded in reloading and brought the weapon up to fire. In a smooth motion, Airl pulled an arrow, drew and fired, piercing the man's trigger hand in the middle of his palm, causing him to drop the crossbow with a yelp of pain. The arrow continued through his hand and disappeared into the shadows of the alley. The man was left with a gaping hole in his palm, white bone slickly shining. He hugged his wounded hand to his chest and vanished into the shadows at a stumbling run.

Airl gestured with his bow in the direction they'd been traveling, and Brigid followed close after him. She tried to ignore the moans of pain from the first man still curled on the ground, and the feeble curses of the second man as he wrapped his vest around the stump of his hand, trying to stem the steady stream of blood, that looked black under the dim light as it pooled on the cobbles.

Brigid followed Airl down several more connecting alleys until they emerged back onto one of the wider streets, paved with large squares of pale stone. Brigid's eyesight improved dramatically, as the lamp stands now stood only a few yards or so apart; they yielded much larger flames that shoved back more of the night and shadows. Brigid knew they were in one of the more affluent neighborhoods of Barwick; there were no shops or stalls anywhere in sight, and no refuse curdling in the gutter. Stone houses lined both sides of the street, nearly all tucked safely behind fences of iron and stone.

As she followed Airl down the center of the street, the houses gradually grew in size with more than two stories and bedecked with columns and other rich ornamentation. "Where are we going?" Brigid asked.

"Out of the city. The Guild will be watching all the gates, so we can't use any of those," Airl said, slowing his pace and allowing Brigid to catch up.

"Even if the gates are watched, couldn't you just kill anyone who tries to stop us? You didn't seem to have any trouble with those street toughs."

"That's all they were: street toughs. If they'd been branded members of the Guild and I killed them, I wouldn't be able to set foot anywhere in the Southern Realm without the Guild hunting me down. I could get us past one of the city gates, but those would certainly be guarded by actual Guild members, and I can't be sure I wouldn't accidentally kill one trying to get past."

"So we're going to leave Barwick by going toward the center of it?"

"Yes. There is one last way out that won't be watched," Airl said, and Brigid could hardly fail to miss the uncertainty in his voice.

"You don't sound very confident."

"Nothing is for certain, save death. Perhaps taxes."

"And if this way is watched as well?"

"I'll think of something. This is hardly the most difficult place I've gotten out of," Airl said, waving his hand dismissively. He paused in front of one of the houses, though Brigid supposed it was large enough to be called a manor and studied it for a moment before moving on to its neighbor, roughly the same size, built of white stone accented with black marble.

"This is the one," Airl said, lifting the latch on the gate and holding it open for Brigid. She hesitated a moment before stepping through and watching Airl close it behind them.

"The way out of Barwick is in here?"

"Yes, in the cellar," Airl led her around the side of the manor, around several thick evergreen bushes carved into elaborate shapes, to a small enclosed garden at the back, though it was very dark, the light of the moon being the only illumination.

"Is it a tunnel?"

"Of sorts. You'll see." Brigid forced herself not to flinch when he touched her lightly on the shoulder, for her eyes had gotten used to the bright lights of the street, and she couldn't see Airl next to her.

"If you close your eyes a few moments, it will help you get your night sight back faster. Stay here; I'm going in to open the back door."

"Break in, you mean. I'm just supposed to stand here in the dark?"

"There's no breaking when I'm involved. Archery is not the only thing I am devastatingly good at. I won't be long, but if any more street toughs show up, just club them with your saddlebags."

"I wish they were still filled with books, so I could club you with them instead," Brigid muttered, though Airl didn't reply, so he must have slipped away.

She felt foolish just standing there in the dark, waiting for a man she'd just met earlier that day and knew next to nothing about, to let her into some strange manor house to flee from Barwick. Since Airl showed up at her door and took refuge in her room, Brigid hadn't time to stop and think. Now she wondered if the whole thing was an elaborate ruse to remove her from prying eyes, so he could do with her as he liked, but then she reflected if that were the case, he wouldn't have brought her so far, not when they passed through any number of serviceable alleys. She also had to admit the men they'd encountered seemed more interested in Airl than herself, lending his tale credibility.

While she considered this, her eyesight improved enough so she could see she stood close enough to the manor to reach out and touch the rough cut stone. The garden around her contained several trees, though it was still too dark to discern much beyond vague shapes.

The single door leading out to the garden opened suddenly, revealing Airl on the other side, a small lamp in his hand. Squinting against the light, Brigid walked into the manor and paused as he shut and latched the door. The lamp he held was of beautifully worked gold, and the stem used to adjust the flame was capped in a red gem that sparkled in the light. The lamp looked to be worth more than her parents made in a year, and Brigid saw another just like it sitting on a low table by the door.

Airl lead her out of the room, which Brigid guessed to be a small foyer, into a wood-paneled hallway wide enough to drive a cart through. Every few yards down they passed a small table with a vase or other doubtless valuable trinket, and Airl lead her past several closed doors until he opened one to reveal a tightly curved staircase disappearing down into darkness.

"Whose manor is this?" Brigid asked, as she followed him slowly down the steps.

"One of Barwick's wealthier merchants. The lady of the house is a friend, of sorts."

Brigid waited a moment to see if he would elaborate, and when he remained silent, she asked, "Does she know there is a secret tunnel under her manor?"

"No, and she's a terrible gossip, so it's good she doesn't, especially considering where it leads." Airl's boots hit the stone as he stepped of the stair, though Brigid stopped three from the bottom. "Where does it lead?"

"One thing at a time," Airl said, holding the lamp high and taking in their surroundings. Brigid saw he stood in a wide open space filled with a huge assortment of items. Much of it was furniture arranged in towering stacks, though she also saw thick bolts of cloth, rolled tapestries, two complete sets of rusty armor and three large chandeliers, each sitting in the midst of a pool of broken crystal that glittered like a field of new fallen snow.

Airl looked about in all directions until he nodded to himself and walked down one of the rows made by stacked furniture. Brigid hurried down the last few steps and followed down the row to find it end at a narrow wooden door standing slightly open. Airl pushed it open with his free hand, revealing a small square room.

Tall shelves displaying dusty bottles of wine mostly hid two walls, and the third wall was covered by a large floor-to-ceiling mirror, perhaps a yard wide and set in a gilded frame. The surface of the mirror was distorted enough Brigid hardly recognized her reflection. The mirror's frame looked quite old to her, though kept in pristine condition and oddly free of the dust that coated the bottles.

Airl grinned broadly as soon as he saw it and set the lamp atop one of the tall shelves so as much of the room was illuminated as possible.

"So, is this secret passage behind the mirror?" Brigid asked, glad for a chance to set down her cumbersome saddlebags.

"No, the mirror is the passage."

Brigid blinked. "What?"

"It's called a Mirrorslide. One of the few relics left over from before the Fall of Edean. We will step into the mirror, walk a distance inside of it and emerge from another mirror in a completely different place in Irillia."

"I've never heard of them," Brigid said, studying the mirror with renewed interest. The frame was covered in vague lines, twisting to form indistinct shapes. As she studied one section, a slight flicker of movement in the corner of her eye drew her attention to another section, and, for a moment, the new lines seemed to form a human skull, but when she blinked, the lines seemed to be a jumbled mess, not forming any particular object.

This happened a few more times in the space of a few moments; Brigid caught the likeness of a bouquet of flowers, a pair of crossed swords and a man and woman in a passionate nude embrace, causing Brigid to tear her eyes away from the frame with her cheeks warming.

Airl, who was inspecting the frame from a closer position, appeared not to notice. "Is it so hard for you to believe something could exist or have occurred without being recorded in a book for you to read?"

Brigid considered making a rude gesture at Airl's back but decided against it. "Hardly." She contented herself with redistributing a few of her belongings in the saddlebags so the weight was more evenly placed.

Airl said nothing in response but continued his close scrutiny. A moment later, he placed one finger from each hand on a spot on the frame and pushed inward at the same time. Brigid heard two *clicks*, and Airl stepped back from the mirror.

The glass rippled from the top of the frame to the bottom and back again, and the ripples smoothed away all the distortions of the glass, leaving behind the most pristine mirror Brigid had ever seen, free from all defect, save one. In the center of the glass, a perfectly round circle of the mirror pressed outward like a coin pressed into a piece of paper, so the shape could be seen from the other side.

Before he could do anything else, Brigid placed herself between the archer and the mirror. "You still haven't told me where it leads."

"Edean," Airl said simply.

Brigid stared at him for a moment with her mouth slightly open until she remembered to shut it. "If this does bring us there, who's to say we'll be able to get out on the other side? Half of that city was supposed to have sunk into the Anidor, and what's left is in ruins. What if the mirror on the other side is shattered or lying a mile underwater?"

"A Mirrorslide is nearly indestructible. You could swing away with a mace at one and not make a scratch. The frame could not be moved from that wall if ten Os'Nurians tried to shift it."

"What about being underwater? I suppose we'll emerge on the other side able to breathe sea water?"

"I know it's not underwater because I've used it before. It's safe."

Brigid raised an eyebrow. "Why did you need to go into Edean?"

"I was coming the other way. A few years ago, the King and I had a misunderstanding, and I had business in Barwick but didn't want him to know I entered the city." Airl said. "Are we to stand here all night?"

"I was supposed to be in a nice, comfortable bed all night," Brigid muttered. She stood aside and watched as Airl approached his reflection, reached out and pressed on the raised circle. The circle slid back into the mirror with another undulation, and he reached out again as if to touch the surface of the glass. Instead of meeting resistance, his hand passed through the glass as if it were a thin sheet of falling water followed by his arm, shoulder and entire body. The glass rippled slightly after his passing, becoming smooth once more.

Brigid glanced at the small lamp, wondering if she should take the time to extinguish it, decided she didn't want to be in the middle of a strange cellar in the dark and pressed her palm to the mirror. It felt like nothing more than dipping her hand into a pool of still water, and, a moment later, she passed all the way through holding her breath.

Brigid took two steps, unable to see or hear anything, but, before she could begin to worry, found herself standing on a large square tile of dull metal that looked old and scuffed by much use. The square was not very wide, just enough for two people to stand shoulder to shoulder. Walls, made of the same dull metal, rose on either side of the square and joined to form an arch a few feet above their heads. Dull light suffused the walls as if the metal itself was softly glowing.

Just behind her lay another wall, surrounded by a metal frame decorated with the same eye-wrenching vague shapes as seen from the inside. Airl stood a few feet in front of her, looking up at the arch of the ceiling. She thought she heard him mutter, "Always thought they made these things too bloody short." He glanced over his shoulder at Brigid. "Let's get to the other side as quickly as we can. Time moves differently in a Mirrorslide than in the outside world." He took off at a brisk walk, though with her shorter legs, Brigid had to move faster to keep up with him.

The way was straight, never curving in the slightest. They walked in silence for several minutes until Brigid noticed Airl's head tilting upwards towards the low ceiling more often than necessary. Brigid smiled to herself and tried to keep her voice as level as possible. "Have you always been afraid of enclosed spaces?"

"I'm not, nor have I ever been, afraid of something as mundane or commonplace as enclosed spaces." Airl's voice wavered ever so slightly, but he did not change his stride.

Brigid smirked and then stifled a yawn. She wasn't sure how much sleep she had during the night, but the lack of it was starting to catch up with her.

Airl turned at the sound of the yawn. "We must get out of the Mirrorslide before we rest. It isn't much further." Airl paused and pulled the saddlebags off her shoulder and hoisted it onto his own. "Just until we leave the slide." Brigid smiled slightly and nodded her thanks.

The pair went on again in silence and, just as Brigid was about to demand they take a breather where they were, she caught sight of a flat expanse of clean, unblemished mirror blocking their way with their reflections slowly becoming larger as their owners drew closer to it. Airl placed his hand on a small round stud set in the center of the mirror and pushed down. The surface of the mirror rippled outward from the stud, and Brigid's reflection became distorted. Airl passed back her saddlebags and stepped through the mirror, fitting an arrow to the string as he went. Brigid followed immediately after, experiencing the same rippling feeling over her skin as she moved. The sharp scent of salt water flooded into her nose as she emerged from the Mirrorslide.

Brigid was unprepared for the sight that met her eyes, and she gasped aloud.

They stood on massive stone slabs that appeared to have once formed a floor tiled in a colorful mosaic but was now covered in cracks and shattered brick. The sound of crashing waves hit her ears, and she realized they stood only a few feet in front of a steep drop off, ending in surging waters. Brigid realized this must have been the Anidor Ocean, and, though she'd not seen it before, the idea of suddenly finding herself in the midst of the ruined city that so few people, aside from the Irillian Historical Society, had set foot in, completely overshadowed a mere ocean.

The mirror frame they had emerged from stood perilously close to the edge of the drop off, and it seemed that the mirror was originally housed in a large building, a good portion of which now resided beneath the pounding waves of the Anidor.

Brigid stood motionless, gaping at the macabre feast of destruction spread out before her. There was not a single, whole standing building in sight; indeed, few rose more than a few stories before ending in jagged rock while others weren't much more than large piles of crushed stone. Deep fissures crossed each other in the wide street before them, and she could see the remains of two large fountains and a stone plinth upon which a statue must have once stood. All that was left of it were the remains of two stone boots.

Airl stood a few paces away, his bow out and arrow fitted. He did not look back to see if she had followed him through the Mirrorslide but stared off into the distance, his head moving back and forth. "This is Edean?" Brigid asked, kicking at a fragment of a stone tile. She tried to keep the disappointment out of her voice, but Airl looked back at her with a raised eyebrow.

"It was called the 'Fall of Edean', not 'The Ever So Gradual and Graceful Entropy of Edean.'" He turned back to his surveying and began to move carefully forward, his bow still drawn.

Brigid followed after him, and they soon had passed out of the crumbled ruin that held the Mirrorslide and started down the street, once paved with smooth cobbles of dark green,   but now crisscrossed with cracks and fissures, some several feet across and reaching down to unimaginable depths.

A thin fog hung in the air, hanging like gauzy curtains untouched by any breeze. The air felt thicker on her face than it should have and smelled of damp rot and interminable neglect. They had left Barwick in the middle of the night, but Brigid could see the sun beginning to set behind the massive wall surrounding Edean, far off in the distance.

As they continued down the ruined street with Brigid trying as much as possible to follow in the archer's footsteps, he said, "It will take us until after nightfall to get to the wall, but if we move, we won't have to spend the night in here."

"I thought there was no way through the wall," Brigid said.

"There isn't a way to pass through; it is over four feet of solid rock without a seam or crack to cling to, thanks to the Os'Nurians who helped build it shortly after the Fall. The builders left a small tunnel passing under the wall, well hidden and securely closed, but I know where it is."

"Once we get out of Edean, what will we do?" Brigid asked, surprising herself by the use of 'we'. She tried to calculate how long it would take to reach Vridian Ford from the ruined city, and arrived at the slightly daunting answer of at least three weeks, as she no longer had a mount.

"Let's deal with one thing at a time." Airl said. They reached the end of the street and found themselves looking into a large open space with the shattered remains of a fountain in the middle. The large stone bowl was split neatly down the center, both halves resting on the ground. A wide swath of brown, dry grass surrounded the space, and here and there amidst the grass stood spindly trees bare of leaf and appearing to be fit for nothing but kindling.

Two streets lead in opposite directions away from the edge of the space Brigid supposed had once been a sort of town square. She had never thought how eerily empty the whole place would be, how everything was still and silent, as if the entire desiccated ruins were holding its breath.

Airl looked down both streets for a moment, muttering something under his breath Brigid couldn't catch. He finally chose the right hand street and started down it, his bow still fitted with a loosely knocked arrow at his side. His eyes flicked from one side of the street to the other as they walked, prompting her to say, "I thought the Ruins were empty."

"They are, or were, upon my last visit," Airl said, his eyes in constant motion. "Never can be too careful."

Brigid shifted the saddlebags on her shoulder for what felt the hundredth time since they'd left Barwick and turned back just in time to see Airl stumble, nearly going down to one knee.

As Brigid ran to his side, she thought he was merely exhausted, but she changed her mind when she saw the grimace on Airl's face. His right boot sat awkwardly in a small depression in the ground made by a piece missing in one of the decorative stones that paved the road. She stood by uncertainly as he stood up, took a hesitant step and winced. "It seems I spent too much time watching for danger and not enough on my footing."

Brigid forced down a smile and a wry remark on being too careful and instead schooled her face into one of concern. "Did you twist your ankle? I might be able to make a splint for you.."

"No, thank you. I think it would be best to find some shelter and rest for the night." Airl looked to the nearby buildings as if sizing them up as suitable places to rest.

"If you really have twisted your ankle, you can't imagine one night's rest will be enough—"

"You'd be surprised," Airl interrupted. "I heal much faster than most." He gestured to a squat two-story building made of smooth gray slate. Brigid moved to slide under the arm opposite of his injured foot, but Airl waved her away with a small smile. "My thanks, but I can manage."

He began walking slowly towards the building with only a slight limp noticeable. As Brigid drew closer to the building, she could see a thin ribbon of gold metal set into the stone above the wooden doors, twisting to form a shape partially covered in grime.

Airl paused at the front doors long enough to slide his unused arrow back into the quiver on his back and draw one of his long, curved knives. He silently handed his bow to Brigid, who was momentarily surprised at the weight of it in her hand. She had lifted long bows back home, and this one weighed perhaps half of one of those but felt just as solid.

Airl glanced up at the half hidden tracery of gold above the door, smirked to himself and pushed the right hand door open. The door made no sound as it opened, which Brigid found odd because of the moisture in the air. The building was dark inside, though enough sunlight remained outside to illuminate one large space, the ceiling some twenty feet or so above their heads. A large mound of broken furniture was heaped in the center of the room, piled over what looked to be stacked wooden crates.

Airl scanned the room for nearly a minute before he was satisfied and slid off his quiver, lowering himself to the floor only a few paces from the open door. He unstrung his bow, carefully storing the coiled bowstring in a small pouch at his belt, though he kept one of his knives out in easy reach.

"What was this place?" Brigid asked, setting her saddlebags on the floor.

"It used to be one of the lesser buildings of the Unbroken Church. Their Grand Abbey is on the other side of the city." Airl said, and Brigid could hardly miss the flatness in his voice. "Still, it should serve as a place to spend the night."

Brigid peered into the dark corners of the building. As far as she could see, the walls were bare and there was little sign of this having been a church, save for the sigil above the door. "Do you not care for the Church?"

"Let us say we've never seen eye to eye. Always thought they were too . . . zealous."

Brigid knew something of the Unbroken Church, at least as much as anyone in Vridian Ford did who occasionally attended services. The Church existed to spread the word of the Eternal, the One True God and Maker, and had rigid stances on certain topics, but she'd never thought of it as zealous.

Brigid unrolled her saddlebags and pulled out her spare dress, slightly wrinkled despite careful packing. Airl was already sprawled out on his unrolled blanket, munching on some dried meat that smelled strongly of pepper. "I've enough smoked venison to last us both a few days, but I should be able to hunt by tomorrow."

Brigid sighed inwardly as she'd never much cared for the tough, stringy meat. "I suppose it will do." She stood up, holding her unsoiled dress in both arms. "I'm going to find somewhere to change."

"I do apologize for not twisting my ankle closer to an abandoned structure with more than one room," Airl said dryly.

Brigid rolled her eyes at the comment but could not repress the tiniest of smiles coming to her lips. It felt as if it were the first time she had done so since the day before. She made her way around the giant mound of broken furniture, trying not to focus too closely on any of the details, in case the pile was also some poor soul's tomb. Dust lay thick and undisturbed on the floor like an untouched field of freshly fallen snow. Brigid continued until she could no longer see Airl behind the mound and took a few paces more to be sure.

She was now near one of the building's corners, and she could see the remains of a mostly demolished stone wall that once formed a small room. Hardly any of the fading daylight penetrated this far back into the building; the clinging shadows were much thicker, but she could see just well enough to avoid catching her feet on anything. She pulled her old dress over her head and folded it neatly. Her linen shift was still damp in places with sweat, but she only had one spare, so she pulled her new dress over her head and was about to head back around the mound to Airl when a metallic glint from the floor inside the broken wall caught her eye.

Feeling curious, she stepped over the remains of the wall and looked for the source of the glimmer, which turned out to be a small brass ring set into the floor, partially covered by a filthy piece of cloth that might have once been a rug judging by the shredded tassels. Brigid kicked aside the carpet and bent to get a closer look. The tarnished brass ring was attached to a small section of the floor which was wood instead of stone. She pried the ring up out of the grime of centuries and pulled upward, not expecting anything to happen.

The section of wood swung upward, revealing a small space underneath. She could see one end of a small box sitting in the space, so she reached in and pulled it out. Brigid rose to her feet, studying the object in her hands. It looked to be a lock box for holding something important,. As she looked closely at the gold filigree tracing around the box, she could see no way of opening it.

Wanting to examine her find in better light, she headed back to their makeshift camp, her old dress over one arm and the box in her opposite hand. Even before she caught sight of Airl, she could smell the sweet, slightly acrid smoke of his pipe. As he came into view, Brigid was unsurprised to find him lounging on one elbow, his injured foot tightly bound in a white cloth. "You certainly didn't have to move that far away," Airl said, watching her return. "I wasn't about to hobble around after you just to catch a glimpse of a girl in a shift."

Brigid silently held up the box so he could see it, and his eyes narrowed slightly. "Didn't your mother ever teach you not to pick up strange things off the ground?" He clamped the end of his pipe in his teeth and took the box from her in both hands. "Where did you find this?"

"Hidden in a little space under the floor. What is it?"

"It seems to be some kind of a lock box. As it belongs to the Church, I should just throw it in the middle of that pile," Airl motioned with his chin at the mound of debris, "but like you, I'm curious as to what's inside." He turned the box over and over in his hands, studying it from every angle. Brigid slid her old dress into her saddlebags and helped herself to some dried meat. It was quite peppery, but she was hungry enough she didn't care.

By the time she had finished and was drinking from a half-full skin, the water flat and warm, the outside light was nearly gone, and Airl still prodded at the box with both hands, trying to persuade it to open. As she watched Airl, a wave of exhaustion washed over her, and she only had time to pull her saddlebags under her head before sleep took her.

When she opened her eyes, she found herself lying in a pool of early morning light, though it took her a moment to remember why she was sleeping on the hard ground in a building filled with a mountain of rubbish. She turned her head and saw Airl sitting nearby with his legs folded beneath him, reading from a long piece of paper that curled at both ends. It seemed Airl had begun reading it not long ago, as most of the paper had not passed through his fingers.

"Did you get any sleep at all?" Brigid asked, trying to coax her hair into some semblance of order with her fingers. Not for the first time she wished she had shorter hair, if only so it were easier to care for.

"A few hours. I managed to get this open last night but couldn't read anything in the dark." Airl continued studying the paper, not looking up.

Brigid stared at the paper for a few moments until she had chased the last remnants of sleep from her mind. The box sat in two pieces on the ground at Airl's side, and she could see more paper wedged tightly inside the bottom of the box. "How did you manage to get it open? Smash it on a rock?"

Airl smiled slightly at this but did not take his eyes off what he was reading. "I was about to resort to that very idea when I finally stumbled across the correct way to open it."

Brigid came over to where he was seated and looked at the paper over his shoulder. The words were written in a flowing, precise hand and also in a language she had never seen. Most Irillians spoke *Common*, save for those who lived in the Drannon Desert, who spoke *Kalsam*, and those who lived on the Pearl Islands far to the south, whose language was *Boshe*. Brigid had seen a few lines written in both of those languages, and she remembered enough of what each looked like to recognize what was written on the paper was neither. "What language is that?"

"It is *Qesryan*, otherwise known as the High Speech of Edean. I'd wager there is a bare handful of people on all of Irillia who could read this, and one of those sits before you."

Brigid waited for him to continue but, when he only slid the paper through his fingers a few inches to reach an unread section, she asked, "What does it say?"

"*Qesryan* was originally intended for very formal occasions, so it takes much longer to say anything in it than if this was written in *Common*. This scroll seems to detail the complete history of the Unbroken Church, starting from their beginning in this very city."

Airl paused and looked down at the remaining paper still neatly curled in the box. "I am more curious about the contents of this second scroll. It seems to be written in some kind of code even I cannot read."

Brigid bent down and pulled the scroll from the box. The paper covered a third object in the bottom of the box, a circlet of gold made of flowing lines and bright as a freshly minted coin. She pulled the circlet out with her other hand and saw two perfectly clear, flawless gems set into the side of the circlet, appearing to rest just over the wearer's temples.

Airl sat rigidly still, his eyes fixed intently on the crown. "It's best if you put that back."

Brigid placed it carefully back into the bottom of the box, and Airl visibly relaxed. "What is that? I don't remember anything in the teachings of the Unbroken Church referring to a crown."

"It's not an ordinary crown. One of the Church's closely guarded secrets is their elite enforcers, Paladins, each wear a piece of jewelry they call the Eternal's Blessing. It pierces their skin and allows them to wield Blood Magic."

"Paladins? I thought the Church was only comprised of Clerics and the Prime Regent."

"As they'd like everyone to believe. Some small town Clerics might not even know of the existence of Paladins. They hail from the Unbroken Citadel, serve as personal guards of the Regent and carry out his will where Clerics cannot."

"How does Blood Magic work?"

"It allows the bearer to perform great feats of strength, stamina and speed. A Paladin can overtake a horse at full gallop, straighten a horseshoe with their bare hands and quickly heal from wounds that would cripple or kill other men. These feats drain life from the Paladins, so they lose years off their lives and succumb to old age and death much sooner than normal." Airl glanced at the circlet and frowned. "Unless I am wrong, that is the Crown of Glory, the single most powerful Eternal's Blessing ever made, and I've no idea why it is here and not in the Citadel."

"Shall we just leave it here?" Brigid asked. "It's been hidden here all this time; maybe the Church has already searched Edean and not found it."

"I'm sure they have, but I don't want to just leave it lying around for anyone to find. I'll keep it with me until I decide what to do with it."

Brigid unrolled the paper in her hands and studied the first few lines, though the small symbols consisting of short lines intersecting at different points was as inscrutable as the twittering of birdsong.

"Couldn't take me at my word," Airl asked, "or did you believe you could glean something from those scratches from something you read in a book once?"

Brigid turned to scowl at his words but saw he was grinning at her. "I merely wanted to see for myself," she said and bent her head to concentrate on rolling up the scroll so she wouldn't have to see his patronizing grin. "Besides, I wouldn't imagine one who spends all his time winning archery contests and collecting trophies could have much time to spend in libraries."

"You are correct to assume I haven't frequented many libraries, though I've known a few librarians who enjoy a drink now and again. Present company excluded, of course."

"I'm sure those librarians never tire of hearing about your endless collection of awards for launching sharpened sticks at stationary targets."

Airl looked about to reply, but then his eyes fell on the open box still in Brigid's hand. He rose to his feet, silently took the box from her and began packing up his few supplies. "We'd best be on our way. We still have much of Edean to cross."

As she repacked her saddlebags, she asked, "After we leave Edean, will you escort me back to Vridian Ford?"

"I have to make another stop first at the Middle Realm."

Brigid nearly dropped the book she was inspecting for damage. "Why? Aren't Azoreans hiding there?"

"Yes, and they need to know the Unbroken Church is marching north in an attempt to attack and destroy them."

Brigid studied his face with a half-smile on hers; the notion was so ridiculous it had to be an odd attempt at humor. He met her gaze steadily, and his expression did not change. "Wait—what?"

"Just before I was accosted in the common room of the *Ledger*, I overheard a group of mercenaries drinking and talking eagerly of the slaughter of Azoreans and how the Unbroken

Church was overpaying for a task they'd gladly do for free. There were no Clerics in sight, though I'm sure none of their pious ilk spends much time in common rooms."

"That makes no sense. I know the Church doesn't care for Azoreans, but I can't imagine them openly marching to slay them. Wouldn't the King or the House of Commons have something to say about that?"

"They tolerate the Azoreans living in the Middle Realm as it keeps them away from everyone else. The Unbroken Church has quietly hired mercenaries in the past to try to eradicate the Azoreans, but they never had much success. So now they are launching a full assault disguised as one of their yearly pilgrimages, though they hardly have to bother even then, as I'm sure you know how much Azoreans are abhorred in both Realms."

Brigid mulled this over for a moment while Airl expertly restrung his bow. She'd heard gossip on the village green that the Unbroken Church was more rigid and fundamental in their own Citadel than what was preached in small towns, but she'd never thought it went that far. "So you decided to wait until now to tell me this?"

"I didn't think you'd care. Aren't you eager to head home?"

"I am, but I'd like to get a closer look at the Middle Realm," Brigid said casually, though the archer's revelation about the Church was troubling. It shattered her image of the benevolent Church, and she took no pleasure from it.

Airl smiled slightly, as if he knew exactly what was swirling around in her mind like water pouring from a hole in a washtub, and pulled his quiver over his head after checking his knives were secure in their sheathes. "We need to be off. I will tell you all I know about the Middle Realm on the way."

Chapter Eight

The next few days passed in similar fashion for Owin. Most Azoreans he shared tasks with were polite and good-spirited, not much different than the townsfolk he had left behind in Vridian Ford. At first, Owin thought it must have been because he was new to the Colony, and the other Azoreans wanted to make a good impression. However, as days passed and their demeanor remained the same, he realized they were genuine. There were a few Azoreans who kept to themselves and walked about with downcast eyes, but none had been so brash as Zaul, and Owin discovered it was relatively easy to avoid him. Zaul tried to corner him a few more times during Owin's first week, but he managed to beg off, using his schedule as an excuse.

About a week since he first arrived, Owin was walking past the small orchard, having just hauled water to the vegetable gardens, and he came upon a very attractive female Azorean he had not met before, standing on a short barrel and tossing ripe apples over her shoulder into a large basket on the ground. A second basket sat next to it, already filled to the brim.

She was at least a head shorter than he with short chestnut brown hair that framed a heart-shaped face. She wore a gray dress cut in a similar fashion to those worn by the other women in the Colony, though with a squared neckline, displaying an admirable bosom.

Owin stood watching her fill the basket with red apples for a few moments, suddenly unsure how to approach her. He could not recall the last time words did not come easily to him in the presence of an attractive woman, but his mind was a blank.

"Can I help you?" the woman asked, not pausing in her picking.

"I'm new to the Colony, and I haven't seen you before, so I thought I'd introduce myself," Owin heard himself say.

"I know who you are, Owin," she said and turned to face him, an apple in each hand. Her eyes were large and dark blue, and the only visible gray patch on her face was a web around her left eye, though from a distance it could easily have been an elaborate tattoo. "I'm Verona, and I haven't time to give you directions. That silly bint Paloma is sick, and I have to pick up her slack." Her mouth turned down at this, as if Paloma's being sick was just a ploy to give Verona more work to do. She tossed the last two apples into the full basket, and Owin moved to take her hand and help her down the ladder, but she took no notice and hopped off, easily landing on both feet.

"Do you need some help carrying these baskets?" Owin would not be so easily deterred and bent down to lift the fuller of the two.

"Hardly." Verona lifted one of the baskets, balanced it on one hip and lifted the basket at Owin's feet one-handed. She handled them as easily as if they were empty. Without another glance towards Owin, she headed towards the mess hall, leaving him to try to recall if he had ever so spectacularly failed in a conversation with a woman before.

To add further insult, at that evening's meal, he made an innocent inquiry about Verona to Meryl and was informed Verona and Zaul were lovers. After learning this, Owin made no further attempt to talk to her, though the next time he crossed paths with Zaul, the Azorean wore a slightly superior smirk that Owin mostly succeeded in ignoring.

Owin had mastered how to block most punches during his training, as well as how to hit his opponent without major injury to himself, though Oriana still claimed in a real tavern brawl, he would not last much past his first opponent. Owin fared much better in his use of his Talent. He was now able to move objects in simple patterns in midair, up to three at a time, and he was also able to hurl objects at a stationary target with some fair accuracy. He continued his run around the outside of the colony just after rising each day and found, much to his surprise, he enjoyed it. Occasionally he was passed by Zaul, running the same circuit and moving so fast he made Owin feel as if he were running backwards.

It was during one of these morning runs Telas spoke directly into his mind, informing him Ox would like to speak with him in his study at Owin's earliest convenience. The two leaders of the Colony shared a study, located in a stone-roofed building in the eastern part of the Colony adjacent to the building which served as the library and a meeting place.

As he passed the library, which doubtless held more books than the small one at Vridian Ford, it occurred to Owin he had not thought for a few days about the home and the family he left behind. He expected to feel a pang of loss as strongly as his first day as an Azorean, and, while the loss was there, it was not so keenly felt like a wound that had begun to close.

Owin stepped into the study, a small round room which was kept stark and very clean. The only furniture was a large desk behind which Ox sat, two chairs facing the desk and a small stand, off to the side, piled with ledgers. The only other furnishings in the room were a large cloth map of Irillia mounted on the wall, flanked by two unlit iron sconces.

The map caught his attention at once, as it was finer by far than the one in the Council's Chambers back home, with fringe at the corners and silver lettering denoting names of cities, villages and rivers. The Middle Realm was represented by a thick black line without a label, just as on the Council's map. Ox read in silence for a few moments before nodding to himself and closing the ledger.

"This is quite a map you have," Owin said, tracing his finger over the words *Vridian Ford.*

"Aye, fine enough for a king's personal chambers," Ox said with a grin. "It is on extended loan to us from His Majesty of the Southern Realm."

Owin found himself smiling back. "I'm sure he didn't miss it at all."

"Oh, he did, from what I hear. Had his personal guard flogged every day for a week when it disappeared." Ox gestured to one of the chairs across from his desk. "Care to take a seat?"

Owin would have preferred to stand and study the map some more, but he circled the desk and sat in the offered chair. "Oriana tells me you are making great progress with your Talent."

"Really?" Owin was genuinely surprised. "She's never said anything like that to me."

"She doesn't want you to get complacent." Ox leaned forward over his desk and lowered his voice. "Between us, she said you're proceeding much faster than she expected." He leaned back in his chair and studied Owin for a few moments in silence, large fingers stroking his chin. "I've decided to make you a Soldier of the Colony."

Owin's surprise must have been plain on his face because Ox grinned widely before continuing. "You'll not have any new responsibilities unless it be to protect the Colony or other Azoreans."

"I'm not much of a fighter, Ox. Oriana could have told you. I'm convinced the only reason I've ever hit her in our sparring matches is when she lets me."

Ox waved a large hand as if shooing away a gnat. "Fighting is not just about being able to hit the other fellow harder than he hits you. If so, I'd be able to defend all the Colony by myself." Ox pulled out a stoppered stone jug and two dented tin cups from one of the drawers in his desk. "Those of us with Talents more suited for fighting are made Soldiers shortly after joining the Colony, regardless of ability. Why, if my aged grandmother could do what you do, she'd be a Soldier too, even though she couldn't throw a punch hard enough to swat a fly. Once you've had some more practice, I'd wager you won't have to worry about anyone getting close enough to punch you again."

He poured a large measure into one cup, a smaller measure into the other and slid the latter cup across the desk. "My own recipe for corn mash spirits. We save the real drink for special occasions, seeing how hard they are to come by." Ox held up the cup in one hand by the handle, his large hand making it seem little more than a teacup. "To the newest Soldier of the Colony. May you never see a moment of duty."

Owin barely had gotten his hand around his cup before Ox tossed his back as if it were merely water. The sharp burn of alcohol filled Owin's nose as he raised the cup to his lips and took a tiny sip. He stifled a cough as he felt it race like fire down his throat. He'd had wine and beer often enough, but those might as well have been milk compared to this. He set the cup down, even as Ox poured himself another measure.

"Of course, I am the leader of our little army, and Zaul is my captain." Ox correctly interpreted the look of disdain on Owin's face. "Aye, he is a pompous ass at times, but he is a vain man, so I gave him the title to be sure he'd stay loyal to the Colony. His speed is worth more than his weight in gold to us."

Owin stifled another cough as he felt the liquor burn its way into his stomach. "Who do we have to defend the Colony from?"

"Anyone and everything. A few months past, a small band of mercenaries crept here in the dead of night and killed a half-dozen Azoreans before the alarm was raised. Last year a pack of wild dogs tried to make off with half our herd of sheep. These things don't happen often, but we Soldiers are there when they do." Ox glanced at the pile of paper in the corner of his desk and sighed. "I'd best be getting to these reports. I don't mind reading, but a man o' my disposition isn't made for keeping ledgers. Thank the Eternal Telas does most of the writing and sums. It's half the reason I put up with her." Ox winked and pulled the pile across the desk.

Owin placed the cup on the edge of the desk, grateful to not have to drink any more, though he thanked Ox for it. The big Azorean nodded in response, not taking his eyes off the top paper, so Owin showed himself out after a lingering glance at the map on the wall.

After a quick stop at the Mess, Owin entered the Pavilion to find Oriana waiting for him, standing next to what looked like an entire pig hanging from a wooden stand. The pig was missing its head with the supporting rope disappearing queasily into the gaping hole at the top of its neck. Shiny bones still pink with blood protruded from the neck stump, and Owin averted his eyes from the sight before he brought up the boiled oats he'd just eaten at breakfast.

"Welcome, Owin," Oriana said, sensing his discomfort and stepping in front of the carcass, partially blocking his view. "I believe I've taught you all I can about fighting with your bare hands; you're not coordinated or strong enough to hold your own in a pitched brawl, so, starting now, we're going to work on using your Talent as a weapon."

Owin rather thought he'd gotten much better since the first day he'd arrived at the Colony but didn't voice his opinion. Instead he said, "So, I'm to practice on a pig instead of you?"

Oriana gave him a flat look with her one good eye. "You wouldn't be able to touch me, Talent or no." She crossed to one of the equipment tables lining the walls and came back with a fistful of knives, all held by the handle so it looked like she held a curled porcupine. Standing to the side of the pig, she casually rammed one of the blades into the pig's exposed belly and ripped it free. Red coated the blade, and a small trickle ran from the wound.

"The pig's had most of its blood drained, but it will still serve as a stand-in for a human body." She wiped the crimson blade against the pig's hairy side, getting rid of most of the blood, and she returned the knife to her fist.

Owin forced himself to look at the pig, gently swaying upon its rope, but tried not to concentrate on the neck stump. "So, this is supposed to make me used to blades going into flesh?"

"Exactly." Oriana said, and she pressed the bundle of knives into his left hand. He recoiled slightly from the blood on one of the handles but still took it. He extracted one of the knives and hefted it for a moment before using his Talent to make it rise out of his hand and hover, quivering, in the air just to the right of his head. He made a small flicking gesture with his fingers as if shaking water from them, and the knife shot into the bottom of the carcass. He'd applied too much force with his Talent, and the knife sank into the sallow flesh of the pig's haunch past the hand-guard.

"You don't need to flap your hand at your target. It takes too much time and gives away what you're aiming for," Oriana said and wrenched the buried knife out of the carcass with a loud squelch which made Owin's stomach twist uncomfortably. As she handed it back to him, she said, "We'll have to see about getting you blades with wider guards."

For the next half hour, he sent one knife after another into the pig's body, honing his accuracy, until he was reasonably sure he could kill an oncoming enemy with a single Talent-thrown blade. When he was done, the carcass was covered over with so many bloody cuts that large swaths of the flesh hung in tatters, revealing glistening muscle and other viscera Owin didn't look at closely enough to identify. He pulled the knives free from the body, leaving it to sway gently from its rope. Blood pooled on the ground beneath it, staining the sand.

Oriana, who'd spent the training session sharpening and oiling a spear taller than she, tossed him a square of clean linen and watched as he cleaned the knives. "I'd not enter any tavern contests, but your aim has improved."

Owin, who tried to pretend not to care, felt a small swell of pride in his chest at her words. It was nice to hear her to praise his progress, no matter how grudgingly given. He finished cleaning the blades and passed the fistful to Oriana, who inspected them critically before setting them back on the table. Owin tried to hand the stained cloth to her as well, but she merely raised an eyebrow at it, so he stuffed it in his pocket. He made a mental note to send all the clothes he currently wore to the laundry as his sleeves and pants had speckles of red on them, despite his taking care while wiping down the blades.

Oriana hefted her spear and slung it over her shoulder like a fishing pole. "That's all for today. I'll speak with Heph and have him forge some blades with wider guards for you."

"Thank you," Owin said and glanced at the pig carcass. "What's to happen with my target?"

"He's to be hung in the rookery for the ravens. They like their meat fresh and uncooked," Oriana said and smiled slightly at the look of disgust that passed across Owin's face. "You asked."

Later that same day, Owin returned to the training room to find Oriana and Zaul waiting for him. Owin paused at the door, unsure if he had misread his schedule, when Zaul moved over to him. Even though he'd seen it before, Zaul's speed still surprised him; it was as if he crossed the dozen or so paces in one step. The only indication Zaul had moved at all was his cloak settling on his back, as if moved by a stiff breeze. "Welcome Soldier Owin! Barely in the Colony less than a fortnight and already a Soldier! Fastest time the Colony's had, other than mine, of course."

Oriana came over, a slight smile on her lips. "I've asked Zaul to help us during your training. You've improved with moving iron from a stationary position; now, I'd like to see you try your Talent on something already in motion." She held up an arrow with a blunted steel tip. "Zaul can move nearly as fast as an arrow in flight, so if you can move this arrow while he is running with it, you shouldn't have much trouble with moving an arrow that's been shot at you."

Owin felt a familiar pang of anxiety in his stomach, and he held up his hands. "Wait a minute. Stopping something falling is one thing, but halting an arrow in flight is another. I really don't think—"

"When you're a Soldier, you often don't have time to think." Oriana handed the arrow to Zaul, who idly tested the tip against his thumb. "You must learn to react first, or you'll have no time to think at all when that first arrow takes you in the throat."

Owin nodded, still unconvinced, knowing further objections would get him nowhere. He was curious to see more of Zaul's Talent as well. He let Oriana lead him to the center of the room, while Zaul amused himself by tossing the arrow up into the air and catching it on the first try, every time. "Don't worry, Soldier; I'll try to go slow for you at first." Zaul became a blur, racing around the edge of the large room, arrow clasped in his right fist.

For the first several attempts, Owin could not even feel the steel of the arrowhead with his Talent. He closed his eyes and located every source of metal in the room and then ignored them all, save the one moving. It took Owin several more tries but finally was able to knock the arrow out of its continuous path around the room, and he heard the thud as the arrow hit the floor.

Nearly an hour and a half later, he was able to seize the arrowhead with his Talent on the first try and hurl it into the ceiling. As soon as this happened Zaul left the room, claiming he had much else to do before the evening meal. Owin barely had time to thank him before he was out the door.

That night, he was walking back to his mound, eager to feel his head hit the pillow, when he saw Meryl walking his way, down one of the rows of mounds that intersected his own. As she drew closer, he saw she wore a dark cloak fastened around her neck and she carried a blanket roll under one arm. She gave him a tight half-smile.

"Where are you off to?" Owin asked as they came to a stop a few feet apart, close to one of the flickering torches that burned all night to give light to those Azoreans going to and from their mounds.

"The Colony Heads have a message they need sent to our sister Colony in the Mossran Mountains."

"That must be over a hundred miles from here! I thought that's why the Colony kept ravens."

"Closer to a hundred and fifty, actually," Meryl said. "This message is quite important, and they don't want to trust it to ravens."

"Why can't they send Zaul? He could be there and back again by tomorrow."

Meryl grimaced at the mention of the fleet-footed Azorean. "He considers carrying messages beneath him. Ox said he wants him close to the Colony, anyway."

"How long will it take you to get back?"

"Around four weeks if they'll let me take a horse on the way back." Meryl unnecessarily smoothed down the front of her cloak. "I'd better be off." She started to walk past Owin, but he stepped into her path and said, "Are you all right?"

"Yes," Meryl said, though she said it so quickly, with forced nonchalance, Owin knew she was lying.

He studied her face for a moment, and she met his gaze stoically. "You can talk to me. You helped me on the worst day of my life; I'd like to return the favor."

Meryl did not immediately refuse his offer, so he forged blindly ahead, latching onto the only thing he'd ever seen bother her. "Did Zaul say something pompously idiotic again?"

Meryl stared at him for a moment, a smile pulling at the sides of her mouth. "You really don't know how to talk to women, do you? Of all the possible things in the entire world that might upset me, you settle on my feelings being hurt by the biggest prig in the Colony?"

Owin clasped his hands behind his back to give himself something to do. "Of course, I do. Many women back in—" He cut off abruptly, seeing too late the vast chasm opening beneath his feet.

"Oh?" Meryl arched an eyebrow. "Perhaps I'll make a stopover in—what was it, Vridian Ford? I'm sure I'll find any number of women with quite flattering stories to tell." She smiled at the expression on Owin's face, try as he might to keep a straight face.

"Go ahead. I'm not—" Owin hesitated for a moment, the sight of the rows of domed huts stretching out behind Meryl bringing the reality of their situation crashing back down. "Nice try. Unless any more Azoreans come from my village, you're not going to talk to anyone." The thought was a sobering one, and Meryl's smile disappeared as well.

Meryl reached out and touched Owin's shoulder. "Thanks for the offer, but I should have already been on the road. Maybe we can talk when I get back?" She reached into her cloak and withdrew a small object tied to a length of cord. She hesitated only a moment before offering it to Owin, palm up.

Owin peered down at the object which darkly reflected the light of the nearby torch. Its surface was dark as pitch with a glassy finish and shaped roughly like a triangle, with the cord looped through a hole chiseled in the center. He took the object in his fingers, and the odd smoothness of the surface prickled at something in his memory.

Owin looked up at her, feeling an unexpected lightness in his heart, banishing some of the somber feeling from moments before. "Is this from the archway—"

"Daart's Field, yes," Meryl said, cheering as she saw his reaction. "I found a piece of it knocked loose several months ago and kept it because it was unique. I want you to carry something from your old life with you. It's helped me." She lightly touched her fabric of her dress over her bosom, and Owin was reminded of the thimble she wore.

Owin blinked several times, successfully holding back the tears that threatened to spill. He grabbed Meryl into a tight hug, her body tense at the sudden movement but then warm and inviting in all the right places. The stone chip was clenched tightly in his fist, the sharp edges threatening to pierce his skin, but he didn't care.

Meryl was the first to withdraw from the embrace. She held his gaze for a moment, her hands resting lightly on his upper arms, before pulling away and continuing on her way to the stairwell.

"Safe travels," Owin called after her. Meryl raised her hand in farewell but did not look back. Owin watched her until the shadows covered her and slipped the cord over his head, resting the stone against his skin. It was warm from its prolonged contact with his skin, though he pretended the heat lingered from Meryl's body. Owin then continued to his mound, where he lay for nearly an hour replaying the conversation in his mind before he drifted off to sleep.

Chapter Nine

Brigid and Airl emerged from the tunnel under the massive wall surrounding Edean at the start of late afternoon, just as the sun touched the tops of the treeline outside of the ruined city. A cracked and pitted stone road lead from the encircling wall into the heart of an evergreen forest, not before traveling through a large meadow overgrown with brambles and patches of wildflowers of every color.

The air at least did not carry much salt tang, and Brigid thought it quite welcome after the thick, stale air of the ruins and the surprising lack of wind, despite being on the coast. The smell of the flowers all mixed together was complex and interesting, though she usually didn't pay much attention to them.

Airl set a brisk pace once they reached the beginning of the evergreen woods, and Brigid kept up with him, ignoring the burn in her left leg that began after a quarter of an hour of strenuous pace.

She wearied of carrying the saddlebags, switching from shoulder to shoulder and never able to find a comfortable spot, but was determined not to ask Airl to share the load. She didn't think he would refuse, but she didn't want to deal with any more condescension from the man.

Airl had been silent since they left Edean and seemed content to remain so, though he had a habit of whistling snatches of songs as he walked which Brigid found annoying, since he wouldn't stick with one until the end but changed after only a few bars.

As night began its slow ascent, he began picking up fallen branches near to the road they traveled on, discarding some while keeping others, after shearing them of leaves and twigs with one of his long knives until he held almost a dozen in his arms.

Brigid opened her mouth to ask when they were going to stop for the night when Airl made an abrupt right turn off the road, tromping into the undergrowth and heading for a clearing several yards off. This left Brigid to pick her way through the bushes and deceptively thin looking piles of dead leaves as best she could, holding her skirt high with one hand.

By the time she reached the clearing, the hem of her dress was torn in three places, and, while they could be easily repaired, she had no needle or thread. She was happy to slump down against the cool bark of one of three fallen tree trunks encircling the clearing, in the center of which Airl was building a small fire with the wood he'd collected.

Once it was going, Airl disappeared back into the quickly darkening trees, muttering something about dinner, carrying his bow and three arrows in one fist. He'd left his quiver propped up against one of the other downed trees, far away from the fire, small as it was. Brigid closed her eyes and rolled her head back and forth, trying unsuccessfully to work a crick out of her neck. She idly wondered if Airl had left his quiver behind to give Brigid a weapon with which to defend herself, though she'd never held a knife with intent to harm someone else.

She opened her eyes and pulled the quiver over to her lap. She undid one of the leather straps holding one of his knives in place and pulled the blade from the sheath with a low rasp. The knife was lighter in her hand than it looked, and the blade gleamed in the firelight as if it had just been polished. The hilt was covered in a tracery of something that could have been a flowing script, though not in a language Brigid recognized, and felt well worn under her fingers.

She spun the knife slowly in her hand, the blade dipping close to her wrist before completing the revolution, as she'd seen Airl do back in Barwick. She spun the knife a few more times before sliding it back into its sheath and securing the leather strap. She straightened the quiver to look like it was untouched and sat staring at the small fire, occasionally feeding it from the small pile of wood left.

Airl came back abruptly into the firelight after a quarter of an hour and startled Brigid to her feet until she saw who it was. Airl carried a pair of rabbits in his fist, each sporting a hole in the head. He barely glanced at his quiver before saying, "Find what you were looking for in there?"

"I just wanted a closer look at your knives," Brigid said, realizing it was pointless to deny it.

Airl sat down next to his quiver, drew the knife Brigid handled and began to skin and dress the rabbits. "I see you looked at *Zelfynn* here. The other is *Zelfynne*."

"I never understood the reasoning behind naming weapons," Brigid said, watching Airl work.

"It adds a certain air of grandeur to them, I suppose." Airl said. "Some folk become so closely associated with a weapon, it's almost as if they've taken on a life of their own."

"I've never heard of anyone naming their weapons, except for Ghent and *Thrazam*," Brigid said, naming one of the famous warriors of long ago Edean.

"I always thought his war hammer deserved a better name than that," Airl said, a fond look flitting across his face before he turned back to forcing a pointed stick through the first skinned rabbit. "Besides, not many men will admit to naming their weapons. A lot of them are named after lost loves, and, if that was known, they'd lose all credibility." He shoved the other end of the stick into the ground, angling the rabbit out over the flames and adding more wood to the fire. "How's it different than naming horses, when you think about it?"

"Horses can recognize their names, and they listen after a fashion," Brigid said.

Airl nodded. "I've never named one. Try not to ride them unless I've a long journey before me."

"Are you scared of horses too?"

Airl arranged the second rabbit over the fire like the first. "No, and there's no need for 'too'; I'm not scared of enclosed spaces."

"Well, you certainly do a good impression of it." Brigid said, grinning. She was reminded of some of the conversations she'd had with Owin when he hadn't been distracted by other women passing by in low-cut dresses. She thought he'd get along famously with Airl, though she admitted to herself she'd be hard pressed to verbally spar with both of them at the same time.

Brigid watched the cooking rabbits for a few moments while Airl poked at the flames with a long stick. She voiced a question she'd been mulling over in her mind since they arrived in Edean. "Who are you, Airl? I can't tell how old you are, and you seem quite knowledgeable about things very few other people on Irillia are."

"I'm Airl, the Greatest Archer Alive," he said, though he didn't meet her eyes. "I'm older than I look, and I've traveled all over both Realms. No offense, but village folk are not known for their expansive world views."

"I would have taken offense if I'd never gone on this delivery by myself, but I'm realizing it is very true." Brigid said. "Still, there's something . . ." She trailed off, not knowing how to finish. There was something in a dark corner of her mind she was reaching for but couldn't quite grasp, a recollection that might reveal more about the archer than he said.

"It's just a personality I've cultivated about myself, a certain rugged mystique," Airl said. He turned both rabbits on their sticks.

The smell of the cooking meat drove the thoughts of Airl's identity out of her mind, and Brigid realized she hadn't had a proper meal in at least two days. Dried venison was fine for soldiers or mercenaries on campaign, but if she didn't eat it again for the rest of her life, it wouldn't be a loss.

The flames began hissing and spitting from the fat slithering down the sticks and dripping onto the crackling logs. Brigid felt her mouth begin to water, and she asked, "Are they almost done?"

"Nearly," Airl said, sticking the tip of one of his knives into the middle of one and observing the fluid that trickled out.

Brigid pulled her saddlebags to her side and opened one of the pouches, more to give herself something to do while she waited than anything else. She unpacked everything and repacked it neatly and found she had more room than she thought. Brigid did the same for the other side and, while there wasn't any more room to be had, at least there were no awkward lumps or sharp corners to dig into her back.

Airl apparently decided the rabbits had cooked long enough for he pulled both sticks out of the ground and away from the flames and passed one to Brigid, who accepted it gratefully. She hesitated, having only eaten rabbit previously in stews and was unsure how to proceed.

Airl took a bite of his rabbit's flank and, while he chewed, pulled off one of the legs and held it by the bone in his other hand. Brigid pulled her rabbit close to her face and blew on the flank before taking a small bite. The flesh was nicely browned, and the meat hot, almost to the point of burning her tongue, but she was too hungry to care. Grease dribbled down her chin, but she ignored it, tearing off more meat with her teeth and gulping it down without much chewing. When she was younger, her father often chided her for eating quickly. She'd often finished her plate before either of her parents were halfway done; however, it had been good practice for this meal, as she couldn't remember being this hungry before nor food tasting this good.

"It's not my best work, but it's passable," Airl said around a mouthful of rabbit. He grinned across the fire at Brigid. "That rabbit's not going anywhere. I don't think you'd appreciate me pounding on your back to dislodge a bone."

Brigid forced herself to slow down, take smaller bites and chew more thoroughly, though she still finished before Airl, setting the remains of the carcass on the ground beside her before taking a long draft from her water skin. She leaned back on her elbows against her fallen tree trunk, enjoying the warm feeling of a full belly spreading throughout her body.

Airl's carcass was much cleaner than hers when he was done, and he tossed what was left into the fire. Brigid leaned forward to throw the rest of her rabbit into the flames, and a belch escaped from her lips before she could suppress it. "Excuse me," she said, covering her mouth belatedly.

Airl smiled. "I think that's the first time I've seen you do something so mundane and normal, Miss Dorcas. It almost makes you seem like any of a hundred other women I've known."

"High praise, I'm sure," Brigid said. She yawned, closed her saddlebags and pulled them behind her head so they rested against the crumbling bark of the tree. "Are you going to keep watch again?"

"Someone has to," Airl said, folding his long legs out before him.

"I can stay up and watch for a few hours."

Airl smiled across the fire at her. "You can barely keep your eyes open. I can survive on little sleep much better than you."

"I might find offense at that if it weren't true," Brigid said and laughed, realizing that she *must* have been tired, finding so meager a joke funny.

Brigid watched Airl take out his long stemmed pipe, tamp some dried leaves into the wide bowl and use a thin stick to transfer a burning ember from the fire to his pipe. The last thing she saw before she closed her eyes and fell asleep was Airl taking long steady puffs on his pipe and watching the small flames of their fire dance the shadows away.

Chapter Ten

It took them only a few more days to reach the Middle Realm; largely thanks to Brigid's having convinced Airl to buy a pair of horses, after several well considered, pointed remarks on their merits and the oddity of being scared of them. Brigid and Airl had to leave the horses tethered to a gnarled oak tree a quarter of a mile from the secret entrance to the Colony. Brigid briefly considered leaving her saddlebags behind, as Airl thought their stop would be a short one but then thought better of it and heaved them over one shoulder, the stiff corner of one of the thicker books poking her in the ribs. Airl carried his quiver and knives over one shoulder and propped his unstrung bow over the other shoulder as if it were a fishing pole.

The entrance was a thin passage cut into the side of a short rocky shelf and covered over with several years worth of green and brown vines. The passage was far too small for the horses, and the top of it nearly scraped Airl's head. For the first dozen yards the floor was covered in dead, slippery leaves, but these gradually gave way to packed dirt.

The passage slanted deeply downward, so much so Brigid was obliged to put out one hand against the rough rock of the walls. She didn't want to lose her balance and go careening into Airl, who had no problem with keeping his balance. All too soon, the light that could filter through the layers of vines vanished, and they continued on in pitch darkness. The only sensation present, other than the rough rock beneath her fingertips, occasionally broken by the slimy feel of moss, was the wet smell of stone and earth.

"Kindly warn me when we get to a turn in the passage," Brigid said, trying to keep her frustration at her inability to see out of her voice.

"What makes you think I would do otherwise?" Airl asked, and he sounded further away than he had before the last of the light faded. Brigid realized she was walking slower than before but could not force herself to move faster for fear of running headlong into something.

"I forget what a limitation it is not to be able to see in low light." His voice was closer now. "If you like, you can take my arm—"

"No, thank you. Just please tell me if I'm about to run into a wall."

"As you wish. The passage continues straight and true; I could shoot an arrow from one end to the other without fear of hitting anything." Airl must have been deliberately scuffing his boot so she could hear how far off he was; she had never heard his footfalls before this. She was grateful for this act of kindness and silently concentrated on the noise, so she didn't have to voice her thanks.

Gradually, the dirt floor beneath her boots leveled out, and Brigid began to see a faint glimmer of light ahead. As soon as the light appeared, the sound of Airl's footfalls vanished. They walked on in silence for a few more minutes, the light brightening with every step. From the steadiness of it, she knew it could only be daylight.

The passageway doubled in width and height until the dirt floor abruptly ended at the side of a deep pit. On the other side of the pit stood an iron grate, studded with rusty spikes longer than her hand. The other side was perhaps ten feet away, and Brigid glanced down into the pit, slightly surprised not to see a bottom. The sunlight, coming from another passage on the other side of the pit, allowed her to see several yards down. There was nothing beyond but unbroken darkness.

A sudden metallic noise startled Brigid, and she leaped backwards from the edge of the pit, looking about wildly for the source. Airl stood against the other wall, having struck a large brass gong that hung in a slight alcove, still vibrating. "Sorry. Should have warned you." To his credit, he did seem sincere, so Brigid bit off the curse she was about to utter. She turned to look beyond the grate to the short sunlit hallway beyond, eager for the chance to see her first Azorean.

Even as the reverberations died away, there was a sudden shifting in the air just on the other side of the grate, and a male Azorean appeared there, a short gray cloak rippling about him as if stirred by a brisk breeze. He had darker skin and slightly tilted eyes, and Brigid could not keep herself from studying the gray mottled patches on his face. The Azorean glanced at her for a moment then turned to look at Airl, grasping onto two thin bladed daggers in sheaths at his belt. "You are not Azorean and, therefore, not welcome here."

"I've been welcomed into the Colony before, though it was—"

The Azorean, who had been studying Airl with narrowed eyes, cut him off. "No unchanged human has ever been welcome among us. Leave now before I add your corpses to those rotting in our bottomless pit."

"Bottomless? How can anyone possibly know that?" Brigid asked before she could help herself.

"Shall I toss you in alive so you can be satisfied?" The Azorean flashed a predatory grin.

"Not unless you go in first to break my fall."

"You're getting yourself into a losing battle there, my friend," Airl said. "She may seem young and pretty enough to sit on your knee in a tavern, but her tongue is as quick as a whip and twice as biting."

"Quick as a whip, eh?" The Azorean looked her up and down appraisingly. "I can run twice as fast as a whip crack."

"Too bad the same can't be said of your wits," Brigid said, beginning to feel annoyed. "Will you kindly let us in?"

"You, perhaps, but your companion is armed."

"I will gladly leave my weapons on this side of the pit, if you would just let me speak with the Head of the Colony. Cedrig, if I remember?"

"Who? We've only had one Colony Leader since I arrived, and it's Ox."

"Oxymandias is the Leader of the Colony?" Airl asked incredulously. Brigid smiled to herself. She had never seen Airl, who seemed to know every little detail there was to know about Irillia, so surprised. "I'm glad to see the Colony still standing."

The Azorean frowned and gripped the hilt of one of his knives. "Be careful of how you speak of our leader, old man. He is a fearless, valiant man."

Airl held up his hands. "I have no doubt he is. When I was here last, he was newly Changed and equally fond of brawling and drinking, often at the same time."

The Azorean gave a sharp nod. "He still is fond of both, but his beloved allows little of either. If you'd leave all your weapons and saddlebags—" the Azorean shifted his gaze back to Brigid, "I will lower the bridge and take you to Ox."

Brigid hesitated, but, after seeing Airl pull his quiver over his head, set it and his unstrung bow on the floor beneath the gong, she followed suit, glad to not have to carry the saddlebags for a moment.

The Azorean moved a few paces away from the grate and pulled on a lever set into the wall. Brigid heard the slow grinding of massive gears coming up from the depths of the pit, and the grate began to lower across the gap until the uppermost spikes bit into the dirt floor on their side.

Airl motioned Brigid to go across first, and she did so, forcing herself not to look down. The image of falling into utter darkness came unbidden into her mind, and she quickened her pace slightly until her feet touched the other side. Airl came after her, as unconcerned as if he were strolling across a meadow.

As soon as Airl was over, the Azorean pulled the lever back up, and the grate slowly rose back into the air. Now that she was closer to him, Brigid studied the intricate patterns on his face formed by the gray patches and tried to do so without staring. The Azorean appeared to ignore her and turned toward the way he had come, as if waiting for something.

Brigid heard heavy footsteps, and a moment later, a very tall, dark-skinned Azorean with a broad chest and heavily muscled arms came around the corner, followed closely by a female Azorean with long black hair flowing down her back. "Ah, Zaul, of course you've gotten here before us," the male Azorean said with light traces of the Pearl Islands in his accent, studying Brigid with interest. "What made you decide—" he stopped abruptly as he saw Airl. He stared at Airl intently for several moments, his large hands slowly curling into fists the size of cobblestones at his sides. "Of all the people to come knocking on our door," he said quietly and thrust forward a finger like a spear, "you'd be the last I'd expect to have the nerve."

This was not the reception Brigid had expected, and she glanced back at Airl, who stood with his arms folded across his chest, the slightest of smiles on his lips. "Well met again, Ox. That little disagreement between us was finished a long time ago, and I am here for quite another matter, one you and every Azorean needs to hear."

Brigid guessed whatever Airl was referring to was more than just a disagreement judging from the thunderhead slowly forming on Ox's face. The female Azorean behind Ox studied Airl with a slight frown as if she were looking for something on Airl's face but could not find it. Zaul stood off to the side, gripping his daggers and shifting his gaze from Ox to Airl and back again, unsure what to do.

"I don't care what reason you are claiming; you can go back across that bridge on your own or I'll—"

"He is telling the truth," the female Azorean said quietly, touching Ox on the shoulder. A note of frustration entered her voice. "Of what, I cannot tell, but he has utter conviction in what he's saying."

"Very good . . .er . . . my lady." Airl bowed his head slightly. "I'd prefer in future if you'd stay out of here though." He tapped the side of his head with two fingers.

With a start, Brigid realized this Azorean's Talent must be the ability to read minds, however ridiculous that sounded. Brigid had of course seen alleged fortune tellers and soothsayers passing through Vridian Ford but never one that had any likelihood of being real. She wondered fleetingly if she could tell if the Azorean was looking into her mind at that moment but then decided she'd rather not know.

Ox turned to the female Azorean, cupping her chin gently in a massive hand. Brigid noticed for the first time the raven-haired Azorean's eyes were of different colors. "My love, this man came to us years ago and, while he did the Colony a great favor, he also—"

"We must think of the Colony first, Ox." She patted his hand and gently pulled away. "Welcome back to the Colony, Airl and companion. I am Telas."

Brigid was surprised the Azorean had not lifted her name from Airl's mind along with his own, but perhaps she had and was merely allowing Brigid to introduce herself. "I am Brigid Dorcas of Vridian Ford." Unsure what protocol dictated and unable to perform a suitable curtsy despite a lifetime of trying, she bowed her head.

Telas glanced at Ox, as if expecting him to say something in welcome, but when all he did was shoot a dark look at Airl, she said, "If you would follow us, we'll all go somewhere more comfortable, so you can tell us your news. I will summon those Soldiers of the Colony not otherwise engaged so they may join us. Zaul, would you please see to it the study is ready to receive guests?"

Zaul nodded once, winked at Brigid and vanished in a blur of motion. One moment he was there; the next, there was no sign of him. As she and Airl fell in step behind the other two Azoreans, she wondered at such speed. Surely there was a limit to how fast he could run, but how could it be measured? What effects did such speed have on his body? She wondered if anyone had ever studied Azorean Talents and then remembered hardly anyone in Irillia knew Azoreans had Talents or cared to know anything about them.

The foursome stepped out of the short corridor which was cut into the sheer stone of the canyon wall. All thoughts on

Azorean Talents vanished as Brigid caught sight of the Colony for the first time. They emerged at the far end of the Colony, and the first thing Brigid saw were the rows of different crops arranged in precise sections, tended by several Azoreans of varying age and ethnicity. As they passed by, one or two of the Azoreans looked up and waved to Ox and Telas but didn't spare a glance for the two visitors behind them.

After the rows of crops, they passed several small buildings, one of which had a chicken coop attached to the side while another was surrounded by a small sheep pen. Brigid had to keep reminding herself not to stare at the Azoreans they passed, though it was difficult; she felt foolish admitting it to herself, but she felt like an explorer suddenly encountering a brand new civilization she'd only read about in books.

The group continued on in silence for a few minutes more until they came to a stone building, slightly larger than the others they'd passed, still only one story tall. Ox held the door open for them, and, once inside, Brigid found one of the last things she'd expected to find in the Colony lining the walls: bookshelves. The collection was small, not much bigger than the one back home and did not fill all the shelves. A round wooden table ringed with several chairs took up most of the room.

Telas bade them to sit, and, after holding out her chair for her, Ox took one directly opposite the one Airl had chosen.

Brigid would have preferred to stand since it was much harder to surreptitiously move closer to the bookshelves to inspect them while seated, but she took the chair to Airl's right.

A female Azorean bustled into the room, carrying a tray laden with a teapot and cups. With the rapidity and grace that comes from experience, she served the tea, leaving the teapot on the tray by Telas' elbow and left the room as quietly as she had entered. Ox reached into his vest, brought out a worn metal flask and poured a measure of brown liquid into his cup before replacing the flask. Telas frowned slightly at this but said nothing.

In a blur of motion, Zaul entered the room, coming to a stop next to Ox, before sitting on the big Azorean's other side and pouring himself some tea.

"Are we waiting on anyone else?" Airl asked, not looking at Ox. "I would think information of this importance—"

"Just a couple," Zaul answered, and Ox glanced at him with reproach. "Owin said he'd attend, but he had a task to finish first."

At the mention of her friend's name, Brigid gave a start but then realized the name was not uncommon, and it surely must be a coincidence. She tried to imagine Owin in such a tightly knit society where everyone had to pull their own weight and almost laughed aloud.

"I think you may want to take it easy on the tea," Airl murmured over his cup. "Seems to me you're plenty jumpy already."

Before Brigid could retort, two more Azorean women entered the room in conversation, but both fell silent at the sight of the humans. One was tall and willowy with red hair gathered in a tight braid, clad in close fitting trousers and a jacket that clung to her figure. She wore an eyepatch over her right eye, and the left, a dark brown, studied first Airl, and then Brigid coolly. The other was short and solid with muscle and had the thickest arms Brigid had ever seen on a woman. She wore her hair short, and she moved with a litheness that belied her size. Her shirt was unlaced at her throat and showed off too much cleavage for Brigid's taste. She sat on Zaul's other side after passing a languorous hand over his cheek and set to studying first Airl, and then Brigid with unabashed interest.

Brigid met her gaze for a moment or two, then blew on her tea, wishing some honey had been brought out. There was another few minutes of silence, save for some slurping noises from Zaul as he drank his tea, and then Telas rose to her feet. "We may as well hear what Airl has to say; I will fill in those not present later." She indicated the one-eyed woman, "This is Oriana." She gestured to the shorter woman on Zaul's left, "and this is Verona."

Airl stood even as Telas sat, and she gave a little nudge to Ox with her elbow who looked up at Airl at last. "Well met. As Ox will no doubt tell you in minute detail, I have been to the Colony before, though it was years ago." Airl proceeded to give an account of the events in Barwick and the impending attack on the Colony. Brigid watched the reactions of the Azoreans across the table as Airl talked, and while Zaul, Verona and Oriana showed surprise and anger, Telas and Ox wore expressions of grim resignation as if Airl just confirmed something they had already suspected. They all showed interest in hearing about their journey through the ruins of Edean.

Airl reached into his cloak, drew out the small box from Edean and set it on the table before him. "We brought you some cryptic missives of the Unbroken Church, as I recalled an Azorean among you who had a Talent for language."

"There was," Ox said levelly, "though she died a few months ago."

"I am sorry to hear that," Airl said. "We also found this in the ruins of Edean, and it intrigued me."

"Never mind about some bloody box," Verona said, turning to Ox. "Have we heard anything about this march against the Colony?"

"Only rumors," Ox said, "like those about the Church openly attacking the Os'Nurians, we thought it the usual horse, ah, leavings." The big man glanced at Telas, who gave the smallest of smiles.

Brigid looked at Airl to see if he showed the surprise at this news she felt, but he only nodded grimly. "I heard those rumors as well, but considering this is the time of year for the Church's pilgrimage, I thought it more likely to be true."

Ox turned to look at Telas, and they exchanged a brief look that told Brigid nothing but probably contained an entire conversation, for Ox nodded and said, "Zaul, I know your feelings on scouting, but you can travel to Barwick and back faster than one of our ravens, so—"

Zaul popped to his feet as if he had springs on his heels. "Speed is needed, and there is no one faster."

"We left Barwick nearly a week ago," Airl said. "I can't imagine the Church would still be there."

Telas nodded. "I'm sure you're correct. Zaul, travel the shortest path to Barwick until you encounter them; a force of that size shouldn't be hard to find. They will doubtless have Paladins with them, so be very careful."

Zaul grinned at this. "I've heard they are very fast. I'd very much enjoy showing them what real speed is." He turned, his cloak flaring out and was gone.

Ox turned to Verona, who was methodically cracking each knuckle. "Please go to Roland's cave and tell him I need to see him."

Verona raised an eyebrow. "Roland? You know how he is about that bloody cave."

"That's why you're going, in case he needs convincing." Ox said. Verona shrugged, drained her teacup in one long swallow and left the room.

"I have asked everyone to gather in the Mess, and I will explain the situation, " Telas said to Ox, rising to her feet as well.

Brigid, who had not said anything since introducing herself, began to feel very unnecessary and wondered if she should have crossed one of the bridges to the Northern Realm and headed for home. She opened her mouth to thank the Azoreans for their hospitality when an Azorean male entered the room in conversation with another short, stocky male Azorean with a close trimmed black beard.

It was his voice she recognized first, and, for a moment, Brigid thought it odd an Azorean would have such a similar voice to one of her friends from home when she looked at his face. It was Owin! A gray patch was over one eye and another slid down his cheek like a raw egg, but it was definitely him.

"Owin?" Brigid stumbled to her feet, barely noticing how high and squeaky her voice suddenly sounded.

Owin froze in mid-sentence, his eyes locking onto hers. All the Azoreans looked first to Owin, then at Brigid. She felt Airl's hand on her shoulder, but she brushed it off and rounded the table, her mind blank for the first time she could remember.

Owin took a step toward her and managed to say, "Brigid, why are . . ." before letting the unfinished sentence hang in the space between them. Owin reached out a hand as if to touch Brigid to convince himself she was real.

Before she could stop herself, she took a step back away from the gray patches on his hand. She tried to say something to cover up her mistake, but she could see by the look in his eyes it was too late. She pushed past the caution and disgust that was ingrained in her since childhood and flung her arms around his neck, even as he took a step back. She hugged him tightly and mumbled how sorry she was into his chest.

She felt his arms encircle her after a moment of hesitation. She let go first and looked into his eyes, grateful he no longer looked hurt but confused. "You better remember this moment until the end of time, Owin Cadmon, because I am never apologizing to you again."

"Don't worry, future generations will be told," Owin said with a wide grin.

"Now you have been reunited, the Colony's needs must be seen to," Telas said as she walked over.

Brigid frowned at her words and expected Owin to say something snide in response, but he only nodded and looked at the Colony Head expectantly. "Ox will fill you in on what you missed. You'll soon see what all that training was for." Telas nodded cordially to Brigid and swept out of the room.

"What calamity have you brought with you?" Owin asked, grinning. "I suppose this'll be the first time I clean up someone else's mess." He winked and moved over to where Ox and Oriana were standing in conversation.

Brigid stared after him for a moment; Owin's time in the Colony seemed to have done him some good. She couldn't remember the last time she had seen him take instruction without issue. Airl wandered over, carrying the metal box under his arm. "Well, it seems they have everything in hand," Airl said, surveying the room. He glanced at Brigid and hesitated, as if choosing his next words with care. "I said I would see you safe to your village." He lowered his voice. "However, now I see the state of their defenses here, the Azoreans will need every able hand that can hold a sword and then some. I don't expect you to stay, of course; I'm sure I can buy a horse from the Azoreans."

Brigid was silent for a moment, watching Owin listen to Ox and then made up her mind. "If I can be of some help, I wouldn't feel right to run away."

Airl scratched at his chin. "I cannot ensure your safety."

Brigid nodded. "I know, but I don't need to hold a weapon. I know something about the treatment of the sick, and I've sewn up a few cuts."

Airl stared at her in silence for a moment, his thin eyebrows nearly touching. "Battlefield wounds are like nothing you've ever encountered. You may know how such a thing is done, but the actual deed will be quite different."

"I know. I will cope with it," Brigid said, proud at how firm her voice sounded.

"I don't doubt your courage," Airl glanced over at the nearest Azorean and motioned Brigid a few paces further away, lowering his voice to barely above a whisper. "No one can be prepared for what one man will do to another in order to stay alive. I have seen more battle than any other ten men taken together, and even *I* am not immune to its effects."

Brigid opened her mouth, and he held up a hand to forestall her. "That aside, if we cannot hold them off, they will surely put every last Azorean here to the sword, and you just for being among them. They may balk at forcing themselves on

Azorean females, but they will have no such qualms taking you countless times without ceasing."

Brigid could not suppress a shudder at his words, and she recalled reading about the sorts of atrocities victorious armies could possibly inflict upon their captives. "If the battle goes that badly for the Azoreans, I can escape the same way we came in." Brigid made a silent promise to herself she would gladly dive head first into the so-called 'bottomless pit' before she let anyone lay a finger on her.

Airl nodded once, solemnly, and the pair crossed over to where Ox still stood, this time in conference with the bearded man who entered late with Owin who was now nowhere to be seen.

Ox frowned slightly at seeing Airl approach but continued his conversation with the shorter man. Before Airl could reach his side, Zaul appeared suddenly next to Ox, the wind from his passage arriving a moment after the Azorean did. Zaul actually appeared winded and was breathing heavily with a grim expression on his face. "It's all true. They are perhaps three leagues away and number in the several thousands. While I was surveying their forces, one of their Paladins spotted me and gave chase. He seemed surprised I outstripped him, but he still got hold of my cloak before I got away. It was my best one, too." He seemed almost as dismayed by this as by the size of the enemy forces.

"Have they any cavalry?" Airl asked.

Ox glanced at him but didn't say anything. Brigid didn't expect Zaul to answer, but he did. "Yes, perhaps a few hundred. The bulk of them are foot soldiers. A lot of boiled leather armor and chainmail."

"Sounds like mercenaries. To my knowledge, the Citadel never had a force of fighting men large enough to mount an attack like this."

Ox finally joined the conversation. "That makes things a bit better. The Church has deep coffers, but all the gold in Irillia will not keep mercenaries in a losing battle."

Airl nodded, looking impressed. "Yes, that was my thought too. Mercenaries often have wildly varied levels of skill and don't mesh well with trained soldiers."

Ox turned to Zaul. "Telas is about to speak with the Colony. Find her and tell her all you've told us." He glanced over his shoulder at the door leading outside. "First, go to Roland's cave and find out what's keeping Verona. Tell her to carry Roland here like a wailing child if they're not on their way."

"She'll enjoy that," Zaul said and disappeared in a blur.

Ox turned back to Airl, giving him a hard stare. "You've decided to lend us your aid, then?" He sounded as if he was trying to resign himself to the notion.

Airl nodded. "We both have. Brigid has some experience with tending the sick."

"Good; we could use her help."

Brigid smiled to herself. She could tell Ox was happier with her help than with Airl's, though she knew the archer would be far more valuable.

"Find Telas, and she will tell you where to go. She'll be expecting you." Brigid nodded and headed for the door. Behind her, she heard Ox gruffly ask if Airl thought the Church would wait for nightfall to attack, and Airl said he didn't believe so, since they have such overwhelming numbers. He continued speaking, but by then, Brigid had walked back outside in search of Telas.

Chapter Eleven

Owin's mind was still reeling from seeing Brigid in the Colony. After the man with his gray hair in a braid pulled Brigid aside, Ox sent Owin to his study to collect the last census that had been done on the Colony as well as the most recent information on the contents of their weapons' cache.

Owin had to pause in the midst of his errand and grinned widely to himself. Maybe he should take Brigid's abrupt appearance as a sign from the Eternal. Maybe things were not as bleak as they seemed. As he found one of the lists Ox asked for, his thoughts turned to the coming attack on the Colony, and he hastened out of the study.

Owin found Ox in conversation with the older man who seemed to be Brigid's companion. From the expression on his face, Owin could tell Ox did not much like the man. As Owin set the papers on the table next to Ox, the other man said, "I haven't ever had to defend from such a unique position before. The Church's strategy will—"

"We won't be fighting from down here in the canyon," Ox said. "Before the Church arrives, we will arrange our defense up on the very edge of the Southern Realm with the Colony at our backs."

"How long do you expect to hold?" The older man asked. "There's nothing but grassland for nearly five hundred yards south."

"The terrain will be altered to help us." Ox answered and accepted the list from Owin with a nod of thanks. "Owin, this is Airl. He is an old friend of the Colony's and has agreed to help in the defense."

Airl gave Owin a slight bow which was returned. "You grew up in the same village as Brigid? When this is over, maybe you can tell me some embarrassing stories involving her."

"She would hate that, so I'd be all too happy to. How did you meet her?"

"At an inn in Barwick, coincidentally the same one Brigid chose to stay at. The Thieves' Guild chose to call in a debt of mine, and, in my haste to leave the inn, I inadvertently involved Brigid. We were chased by men hired by the Guild, and we took a Mirrorslide to Edean. Now, here we are."

"You went to Edean?" Owin asked, trying to conceal a smile. "I thought the wall around it was impenetrable."

Airl gave Owin a flat look. "I was beginning to think Brigid's misconception if she hasn't heard of something before it must not be true was just her personality, but maybe everyone from small villages suffers from it."

Before Owin could come up with an indignant reply, Ox stepped in. "Every Azorean in the Colony can swing a sword or shoot a bow. We have enough blades to go around, but only forty or so bows, so we—"

The outside door opened, and Zaul and Verona entered, followed by a very thin, tall male Azorean with shoulder length black hair. "Finally!" Ox beckoned the three Azoreans over.

"He says he was asleep and didn't hear me knocking," Verona said with a glance at the taller Azorean, who shrugged but remained silent.

Ox didn't reply to Verona and turned to Zaul. "Get yourself some food, get fitted out for battle and then do a scouting run. I want updates on their location every quarter of an hour until they reach the edge of the field."

"I checked on their progress while Verona was walking back with Roland. I estimate their arrival in less than two hours."

Ox nodded. "Try not to tire yourself out before they arrive."

Zaul smirked, winked at Verona and disappeared in a blur.

"Verona, please go to the armory and distribute arms and armor. Telas just dismissed the Colony, so most of the Azoreans will be headed that way."

Verona nodded and left, muttering under her breath as she went.

"Owin, go with her and bring all the archers up to the plain. Airl and I will head up there now, so Roland can have the fortifications finished by the time the archers are ready."

Owin hurried after Verona, beginning to feel his heart beat faster with anticipation. An attack on the Colony was imminent, and he was going to be part of it. As he watched Verona effortlessly lift the large boulder blocking the entrance to the armory, Owin's thoughts turned back to Brigid. He was sure she had enough wits to stay as far from the actual fighting as possible, but he was equally certain if he did something as innocent as telling her to stay out of the fight, she would demand a place up in the midst of the defense.

The armory was located in one of the larger caves set into the side of the canyon face, and, once he followed Verona inside, Owin was surprised by the sheer amount of arms lying in wait, all lying in bundles wrapped in oilcloth or sprouting from stout barrels like deadly bouquets. As Heph was the only blacksmith in the entire Colony, it made sense many of the helms and shields stacked neatly on wooden shelves bore crests from various estates and cities of both Realms.

The first Azoreans to arrive were those trained as archers, and they all wore padded leather armor and iron caps of various makes. A nervous energy seemed to crackle between the archers as they strung their bows, and Owin saw more than a couple excited grins of those itching to finally have something to aim at other than a target.

The other Azoreans receiving sheathed swords or polearms and shields, were much more subdued. Most wore mismatched bits of armor, while the only protection for some was a shield or the iron cap on their heads. Owin knew every Azorean there had gone through basic training with arms, but many Azoreans looked blankly at their weapons as if not sure what they were doing in their grasp.

"It's not as grim as all that," Verona shouted to the crowd as she emerged from the armory, carrying a stack of battered shields. "If those goat-kissing mercenaries make it to you, just remember to hit them with the sharp end!"

Some of the Azoreans grinned at this, but not many. Verona muttered something under her breath as she went back into the armory for more swords. Owin buckled on his belt holding four sheathed daggers with over-sized crossguards Heph made special for him and lead the group of archers toward the southern stair. He was glad to be away from the pervading mood of slow-boiling fear surrounding the other Azoreans.

Owin wore supple leather armor overlaid with chain mail, and he was pleased to find it wasn't as heavy as he expected, though he began to notice its weight on the climb up. The armor left his arms bare, and while he'd found a pair of reinforced bracers that fit well enough, he would have preferred to enter battle with more of his body covered. None of the dozen or so caps or helmets he'd tried seemed to fit properly, and in the end he decided unimpeded vision was more important, so he'd abandoned the search.

When he finally reached the top of the stair, he found a wall of solid, rough rock laid out in a wide half circle completely surrounding the staircase and leaving clear a space perhaps a little larger than the mess hall. The wall looked to be at least fifteen feet high and had a single ramp of stone leading up to a walkway guarded by a flat-topped parapet. The rock was of various hues and textures, appeared to be seamless and was still covered in a thick layer of dirt. Ox stood on the walkway in full plate armor, and Oriana stood a few feet away, leaning on a spear tipped with a foot of sharpened steel.

Airl stood at the base of the ramp with a longbow in hand and gathered the Azorean archers around himself to give out instructions. Owin saw Roland sitting on a small rocky outcrop, his long legs crossed under him, hands on his knees and eyes closed. Owin watched him for a moment, not sure if he was awake or asleep, when Ox called Owin up to the walkway.

Owin walked up the ramp, still feeling winded after the long climb. He saw a double-headed ax with curved blades resting against the wall next to the Colony Head who also had a two handed broadsword strapped to his back. With the full plate armor and the sword, Ox must have been carrying in excess of a hundred pounds on his back, but he moved as easily as if it were a wool cloak. Ox glanced over the courtyard within the wall of stone to where Roland was seated. "Can you make the parapet another foot higher?"

Roland did not move or speak, but a moment later, the whole stone wall shook, sending up a cloud of dirt and rock dust, and the top of the wall stretched upward. "Roland's Talent gives him control over stone and earth. I have no idea how we'd defend the Colony without him," Ox said and motioned for Owin to join him at the parapet.

Owin looked out over the vast field that bordered the Middle Realm, and for a moment, allowed himself to enjoy the feel of the breeze and the sun upon his face, two sensations that were much more subdued on the floor of the canyon.

The field was mostly just flat grassland with the occasional bush or thicket. He shaded his eyes with a hand and could barely see a large copse of trees on the horizon.

"If I were them, I'd gather my forces just behind that treeline before they attack," Oriana said.

"Aye, that was my thought as well," Ox said. "According to Zaul, they have no siege weapons or towers with them; they won't be expecting this wall." He patted the rough stone with a gauntleted hand.

"Shouldn't take them too long to fashion ladders," Oriana mused.

"Ladders we can deal with," Ox said and glanced at Owin. "I wonder what other tricks they may try to breach this wall."

"Never underestimate a Paladin." Airl joined Owin and the other Azoreans, looking out over the plain. "You ever fight one, Ox?"

Ox shook his head, still studying the far off copse as if he could count every soldier of the enemy to a man. Owin took the opportunity to ask Airl what a Paladin was.

"They are the elite troops of the Unbroken Church. Totally dedicated and zealous to a fault, and they use Blood Magic, which greatly enhances speed and strength. I've seen one Paladin outrun a horse at full gallop, and another lift a boulder the size of a wagon wheel. Fortunately, the Church doesn't have many of them."

Ox nodded. "Zaul reported counting seven or eight of them, and they all wore white leather armor overlaid with brass ring-mail. Are my archers ready?"

"Yes. I've instructed them to volley until the wall is breached and then to sight individual targets."

"So long as they don't skewer one of us by accident," Oriana muttered.

"As to that," Airl said, "I took measure of a few of their arrows and, if the whole lot is like that, they won't be flying altogether straight and true."

"The Colony does not have a fletcher. Those arrows were liberated from a shipment headed to the Halls of Woodenouth," Ox said.

Owin heard the tramp of many feet on the wooden stair leading to the valley floor. Perhaps thirty armed Azoreans swarmed into the courtyard, led by Verona. She wore similar plate armor as Ox and carried a large war hammer nearly as tall as she. This new group of Azoreans moved to stand in front of the archers while Verona climbed up to the parapet.

With so many bodies in the enclosed space, Owin could see they wouldn't have much room to maneuver. Most of the Azoreans stood silent, and the air felt thick with crackling tension. Many faces bore expressions of grim determination, though more than a couple wore their fear unashamedly out in the open. Owin tried to keep his expression as neutral as possible; perhaps, if the fear had no outlet on his face, he could remain brave as long as he needed.

Everyone on the top of the rampart stood in silence, watching the grove of trees and feeling the minutes stretch longer and longer. The only sound was the wind blowing gently across the field or the occasional creak of leather as one Azorean or another shifted down in the courtyard. Owin tried to gauge the time of day by the position of the sun, which he had never been especially good at. He had not eaten anything for his midday meal and was beginning to feel hungry, which served to tell the time of day more accurately than anything else.

"There!" Oriana pointed across the field.

Owin looked up, expecting to see a line of marching soldiers and was surprised to see only one person on horseback galloping toward the Azorean fortification.

Airl drew a shaft from his quiver and nocked it but did not draw. Verona glanced over at him. "It's one man on horseback."

"It's one *Paladin* on horseback," Airl corrected. "If he gets within ten paces of the wall, this one's going in his left eye."

"You're going to hit a moving target that small from ten paces?" Verona asked with a sneer. "Fancy yourself another Beowyn the Bowman, old man?"

Airl muttered something under his breath Owin failed to catch. Verona seemed to have heard, as she scowled at the archer before turning back to watch the messenger.

The Paladin pulled his horse up sharply perhaps fifteen yards from the wall, sending up a shower of grass and dirt. He wore the white leather armor Zaul had described and seemed to carry no weapon. He studied the stone fortification for a moment before he spoke. His voice was louder than it should have been, and Owin figured everyone down in the canyon could hear him without much trouble. "Azorean rabble! For too long we have allowed you to sully Irillia with your presence, but no longer! Our beloved Regent, may the Eternal smile upon him, would meet with you to discuss terms of surrender! Send forth a party of no more than five, and he will meet you halfway down this field. As an act of good faith and benevolence, he will only be accompanied by one other. What say you?"

Verona began to mutter a string of curses under her breath, and Oriana and Airl both turned to Ox and began talking at the same time. The big Azorean held up his hand and closed his eyes for a moment, and Owin knew he must be in silent conversation with Telas, wherever she was.

Airl studied the man on horseback with one eye closed and pulled on some of his bow's tension. "I can take him through the throat from here. Not as neat as through the eye, though."

Ox opened his eyes and pulled on his helmet. "Right. Zaul, Owin: with me. The rest of you: stay on the rampart." Verona began to protest but was quieted by a look from the Colony Head. "Telas will have command if we do not return."

"Why do you want me to come?" Owin asked. "If it turns into a fight—"

"Telas suggested it. She thinks your Talent may give us some warning if things are not what they seem."

Owin was not sure he could do anything of the kind, but Ox was already halfway down the ramp with Zaul at his heels. Owin followed after, not without the pit of fear in his stomach growing in size. He was surprised to find Airl following a pace behind. Before he could ask, Airl said, "I have had dealings with the Church before. Besides, Ox doesn't command me."

Ox and Zaul stood close to the east wall of the fortification, near where Roland still sat with his eyes closed. When Owin and Airl joined them, Ox raised an eyebrow at Airl but said nothing, instead turning to look at the seated Azorean. "Roland, we need access to the field, please."

Roland gave no sign he heard the request, but, a moment later, a small section of the wall began to shudder and then sink into the ground, rock chips flying and a cloud of dust obscured

Owin's vision before he thought to throw up an arm in front of his eyes to protect against flying shards.

When the tremors in the ground stopped, Owin uncovered his eyes to find a small opening in the rock wall, wide enough for one person at a time to pass through, though Ox had to shuffle sideways because of his bulky armor.

The Paladin on horseback waited until all four were out on the field before turning his horse and trotting back to the trees. Ox lead the way, Zaul easily keeping pace next to him, and Owin and Airl brought up the rear. The big Colony Head left his massive ax behind on the battlements but still wore his broadsword. The other three were all armed, though Owin still felt foolish with his simple daggers and wondered again why he had been included.

Ox and Zaul exchanged a few brief words Owin did not catch, and then the pair fell silent. Owin looked ahead to the coppice of trees, saw two riders emerge and start towards them at a gallop. The pair passed their compatriot without pausing, and Owin was just beginning to think they meant to ride the four of them down when the riders pulled their mounts to a stop some ten yards away.

Both riders dismounted after checking that the large wicker panniers, hanging just behind each saddle girth, were secure. The panniers' lids were held in place with thick belts of black leather and polished silver.

One rider remained with the horses, holding their leads in one hand while resting the other on the pommel of the sword at his side. The other man, clad in white plate armor edged with gold, strode towards the Azoreans and Airl, a brilliant white cape snapping behind him. His face was thin to the point of gaunt and completely hairless, and his eyes were the dark blue of the middle of a candle flame and burned with as much intensity. Owin had to stop himself from taking a step back as the man's gaze swept over the Azoreans.

When there was perhaps three paces between himself and Ox, the man came to a sudden halt and held up a gauntleted hand, palm outward. "That is close enough, Azoreans." Somehow he managed to imbue that single word with contempt and hatred enough for a tirade of insults and curses.

"Why have you called us here, Paladin?" Ox asked, looking down at the other man with a sneer of distaste.

The rider with the horses took a step forward, his grip white-knuckled on his sword hilt. "Curb that insolent tongue, blasphemer! You have the distinct honor of addressing Loric Exenton, Regent of the Church and more worthy than all Azorean filth ever spawned," the man said, and Owin was surprised at the total and utter conviction in his voice.

"Speaking of blaspheming," Airl said, "doesn't the Eternal frown upon the killing of innocent children?"

Loric waved his hand even as the other rider ripped his sword free from its scabbard with an oath, and the rider bowed his head and remained where he was but did not re-sheath his weapon. Loric glanced at Airl for a moment, eyes narrowed, as if he were trying to decide whether or not to reply. "Shameless Azorean propaganda," he said quietly.

"I have dealt with a few of your predecessors, Regent," Airl said. "We both know what is piercing your chest," Airl tapped a spot on his own chest, just over the heart, "and, more importantly, how it was made."

If Owin hadn't been watching Loric's face, he would have missed the slight widening of his eyes. "You dare to impugn the reputation of a Regent? That is nothing more than a vicious lie only the depraved Azorean mind could conjure." Loric turned back to Ox. "You will hand over to us every member of your Colony with any Talents. They will be questioned and then killed as blasphemers against the Eternal. All other Azoreans will be taken prisoner and removed from the Middle Realm. These are my terms. I will accept nothing less, and, if they are not met, we will slaughter every Azorean in the Colony and cleanse the canyon with fire. What say you?"

While Loric was speaking, Owin found himself wondering why the Regent would need to bring such large panniers to discuss terms of surrender. He thought it likely to be something with which Loric would use to try to kill them, once Ox refused his demands, and, most likely, even if he didn't refuse. Owin closed his eyes and concentrated his Talent on the panniers and was not surprised to find several sources of metal in each.

Using a technique he had only recently begun to explore with his Talent, he probed and traced the largest piece of metal in one of the panniers, trying to guess what the object was by drawing the same shape in his mind. The object proved to be a crossbow, loaded and ready to fire. Owin inspected the other panniers with this technique and discovered each one held a crossbow loaded with a broad-tipped arrow.

All four arrows were pointed downward as if they had not yet been brought up to fire. Owin took hold of the triggers of all four crossbows and opened his eyes to find Ox about to reply to the Church's terms. Owin pulled all four triggers at the same time, and four broadhead points tore through the panniers and embedded themselves deeply in the ground, eliciting several muffled gasps of surprise from within. A small hand stuck out of one of the ragged holes in the bottom of one of the panniers and tried futilely to grasp the embedded shaft to pull it free.

One of the arrowheads must have cut into one of the horse's legs on their short flight into the ground, for one of them gave a cry and reared back, pulling his reins free out of the surprised rider's grasp. He tried to take up the reins again but was having trouble as the horse was still rearing and snorting.

Loric did not turn around, though his lips thinned into a line and his right hand curled into a fist. Ox drew his sword smoothly and pointed the tip of the blade at Loric. "I'm sure the Eternal would not approve of such cowardly tactics, forcing children to shoot us in the back. You will not set foot in the Colony. Those are my terms." His voice was as hard and unwavering as stone, and Owin felt a swell of pride in his chest, suppressing some of his fear.

"I will kill you last, Azorean filth, so you may watch as each and every one of your fellow blasphemers are put to the sword before you." Loric ignored the sword point hanging in the air less than a yard from his face and spoke calmly, though his eyes blazed with hatred.

"Back to the Colony. Now." Ox said, not taking his eyes off the Regent, his sword steady in his hand.

Before either Zaul or Owin moved to obey his command, an arrow shaft seemed to blossom out of Loric's left eye, and he stumbled back with a grunt of surprise, somehow keeping his feet. Owin threw a glance over at Airl, who stood with another arrow knocked to the string and utter calm on his face.

A trumpet sounded from deep within the cluster of trees, clear and long, and a troop of perhaps two dozen archers burst from the shadows of the trees and out onto the field, long bows in hand. Zaul disappeared in a blur, though Owin found himself suddenly rooted to the spot as he watched Loric reach up and pull the arrow from his ruined eye as easily as picking straw out of his hair. The blood flow had already stopped, and Loric seemed to pay it no mind as he cast the arrow aside.

"Owin, move!" Ox pushed him to start him moving, and Owin began to run away from the man who calmly shrugged off what would have been a mortal wound to anyone else. Airl was running full out across the field at a speed Owin knew he couldn't match, and Zaul was no longer in sight.

He could hear the pounding of Ox's heavy boots just behind him, and a breathless muttering that must have meant he was in wordless contact with Telas. Owin risked a look over his shoulder.

The archers formed a single line, each arrowhead tilted at exactly the same angle, and released as one. Owin paused and watched the arrows arc upwards and then begin their descent. He reached out with his Talent and nudged each one slightly, so the arrows veered wildly off course, hitting nothing but dirt.

Another volley lanced toward him, and he pushed these off course as well and started running again. Owin had barely gone half a dozen paces before he heard the third barrage whistling through the air towards his back. Without stopping or looking, he lashed out wildly with his Talent, feeling for the metal in each arrowhead and shoving it to one side, not bothering with conserving his strength as he did for the first two fusillades. None of the arrows met their mark, though he listened carefully for another volley as he ran.

As Owin and Ox neared the looming stone walls, he silently thanked Oriana for pushing him to run every day, since he knew he would have been winded long before reaching safety if she hadn't. As it was, he was less than fifteen yards from the small opening in the side of the stone battlements when Ox bellowed for Owin to get down.

Owin threw himself into a dive to his right without a thought, even as Ox dove to place his armored body between Owin and the oncoming threat. Before Owin hit the ground in a roll, he heard a loud impact of metal against metal and a low grunt of pain from Ox.

Owin completed his roll to his feet and saw Ox climbing unsteadily to his, levering himself up with the aid of his broadsword. Owin saw a large dent scored into the metal between the shoulder blades of the big man's cuirass. A large war hammer with a head the size of a loaf of bread lay a few feet away in the grass.

Owin looked back the way they had come to see if there was anything else headed for them he could affect with his Talent. The only thing in sight was Loric running straight towards them, not as fast as Zaul, but nearly as fast as a horse could gallop. Owin reached out with his Talent to seize hold of Loric's armor and hold him in place, but the Regent was moving too fast and was on top of them before Owin could do anything besides try to get behind Ox.

Without slowing, Loric scooped up the fallen war hammer as if it weighed no more than a wooden switch and swung underhand at Ox, as the big Azorean was reaching for his sword hilt. The head of the war hammer connected with Ox's chest, lifting him off his feet and throwing him into the side of the stone battlement. His impact knocked loose a shower of dirt and pebbles that still clung to the side of the stone from when it was drawn from the depths of the ground.

Loric paused to watch Ox climb slowly to hands and knees, a triumphant smirk on his lips, and, in that moment, Owin grabbed hold of every bit of metal in the Regent's armor with his Talent and pulled him up into the air. Sweat popped onto Owin's brow; he had never lifted anything so heavy before, and it was a strain to lift Loric even a few yards into the air.

The Regent hurled curses down at Owin from his lofty height though he could do little else. Owin ripped the war hammer out of his grip, let it fall to the ground and then shoved Loric as hard as he could with his Talent. Loric flew nearly half the distance back to the cover of trees before disappearing behind the oncoming advance of his footmen.

Despite the certain death that was swiftly closing the distance between them, Owin doubled over where he stood, putting his hands on his knees and taking several deep breaths as he felt the blood pound in his ears. Dark spots popped at the edge of his vision. Owin felt a large hand on his shoulder and straightened up to find Ox standing next to him, his armor covered in dirt and his chest plate dented.

Even as Owin straightened up, a flight of arrows soared over the battlements, headed for the oncoming footmen. "We've got to get back inside," Ox said, wincing slightly as he spoke.

Owin glanced back at the wall of footmen bearing down on them, too numerous to count though close enough for him to see the sigil of the Church emblazoned on the chest of each man. "Don't have to tell me twice."

They ran around the side of the battlement to the section of rock that still yawned open. Ox shook his head from side to side as if to clear it. "Never been hit that hard before," he muttered, almost sounding impressed. Owin followed him through the opening in the wall which began rising back up even as his feet hit the courtyard. Ox paused, passed his gauntleted hand over the indentation in his chest plate and winced. "Feels like the bastard bruised some ribs." He headed for the ramp leading up to the rampart, the gathered Azoreans with their varied weapons parting respectfully before him and several clapped him on the shoulder as he went by.

Owin hurried to keep up, still feeling winded from the large use of his Talent. Sweat poured down his brow which he tried to wipe away on his arm. "I need you up here. Their archers will be in range any moment, so send every arrow you can off course," Ox said, tightening the leather straps on his gauntlets as he went.

Owin nodded, though Ox was ahead of him and didn't look back. Owin felt a small thrill of pride Ox trusted him to do what was necessary, and he would. He knew every arrow he knocked aside was one more that couldn't harm himself or the other Azoreans, so it was a task he'd perform with pleasure.

As he reached the parapet, another volley of arrows soared overhead and fell among the mass of mercenary footmen who were now breaking about the base of the stone fortification like a crashing wave against a boulder. Owin had never seen so many people in one place before, and more were flowing across the field every moment. The momentary thrill of pride vanished at the sight, being replaced by a small lump of ice in the pit of his stomach.

The full weight of the situation came crashing down on Owin's shoulders, and he nearly stumbled where he stood. The lump of ice doubled in size. A part of his mind screamed at him to run, dash down the stairs and take refuge in the darkest place he could find. For the briefest of moments, Owin allowed himself to consider running and then ruthlessly stomped on the thought as he saw the other Soldiers of the Colony standing on the rampart. They watched the deadly mass of their enemies with calm faces and stiff backs, and Owin stiffened his resolve. He would stand and fight for his home, even if it was the last thing he ever did.

Many siege ladders were headed for the wall, made of rough-hewn wood, each at least twenty feet tall and carried by seven or eight men. The enemy archers remained in position behind the bulk of the mercenary horde, still within bow shot, and began to send wave after wave of arrows up over the battlements. Owin began striking out with his Talent at each successive wave of arrows, nudging dozens of shafts off course at a time. Many arrows passed over his head, but he didn't have time to spare a glance over his shoulder.

Airl stood off to the right, nearly at the point where the stone battlements began to curve back towards the canyon. He let loose one shaft after another at a swift, precise pace. He must have been aiming exclusively at the enemy archers for after several volleys from the enemy, the number of arrows sent over the wall began to dwindle in number.

The siege ladders reached the base of battlements and began to swing upwards to rest against the top of the parapet when Oriana leapt to meet their arrival. She wore a round shield strapped to the same arm in which she held her spear and a fierce grin that tugged at the scars around her covered eye.

Owin saw light coursing through Oriana's body, illuminating her skin from within, seeming to follow the tracery of her veins. She pulled off her eye patch with her free hand, and a thin stream of fire leapt from her uncovered eye socket and washed over one of the oncoming ladders, setting it ablaze like a huge torch. The ladder clattered against the battlements and sat there aflame, its handlers abandoning it.

Oriana turned and sent another gout of flame at a ladder that had just come to rest against the battlement, not far from where Owin stood. He could feel the heat from the flames as they eagerly consumed the dry wood of the ladder and saw Oriana's face was drenched with sweat, though she gave a wordless shout of triumph as she set fire to a third ladder, deflecting an errant arrow off her shield as she did so.

There were too many ladders for her to stop by herself; however, while she set fire to a fourth ladder, five more ladders thudded into place, and mercenaries began to swarm up them. Verona shoved one of the ladders off the wall with the head of her war hammer while Zaul ran balanced atop of the lip of the parapet and kicked away three more. Oriana shot a stream of fire at the last ladder, engulfing the mercenary nearest the top in flames, and he leapt off with a scream.

All this time, the Azorean archers continued to send wave after wave of arrows over the wall, though these too had declined in number, as each Azorean ran out of arrows. Scores of mercenaries lay dead or wounded on the field, but they were largely ignored by their brethren, who stepped over their prostrate forms to press closer to the battlements.

The sound of metal ringing off stone came suddenly from the far side of the battlement, and Ox, who was closest to the sound, risked a quick look over the side. An enemy arrow skipped off his pauldron before he pulled back and yelled, "Three Paladins are trying to knock a hole in the wall!"

Zaul, who had been doing circuits atop the lip of the parapet to dislodge any more ladders, vanished over the side. Owin ran over to the side of the battlement and peered down through a small fissure in the stone. Two of the Paladins took swings at Zaul, their war hammers moving inhumanely fast, though Zaul dodged each swing with ease. The third Paladin continued beating away at the rock face, sending up a shower of shattered stone with each blurred swing.

Owin reached out with his Talent, seized hold of all three hammers and ripped them from the Paladins' grasp. He sent them spinning away over the multitude of mercenaries, and each Paladin took off in a different direction while Zaul ran up the vertical face of the stone battlements, certainly a feat Owin might have admired had Ox not bellowed, "They've breached the wall!"

Owin felt his heart leap into his throat as he pulled two of his daggers free and turned to see mercenaries pouring over the wall from three different ladders with two more rising into the air. Verona and Oriana flowed among them: Verona taking wide swings with her war hammer that produced the sound of bones breaking with each connection and Oriana, eye patch back in place, darted about with her long spear. The air was filled with screams and droplets of blood flying like fine mist.

Ox rushed into the fray with a bellow, knocking three mercenaries off the top of the rampart and onto the courtyard below where they were set upon by the waiting Azoreans. A man with a notched sword and missing teeth came at Owin, who used his Talent to thrust one of his daggers into the man's neck and pulled it back into his hand as the man crumpled. Owin tried to ignore the blood dripping down the blade as he moved closer to the melee, looking for an opening.

Two mercenaries tried to move around the brunt of the battle by balancing on the top of the parapet as Zaul had, but Owin pushed against their ring mail with his Talent, sending both over the edge. Ox was a fearful sight, laying about him with his broadsword in one hand and seizing mercenaries by their throats with the other, hurling them back over the parapet. Verona faced a Paladin who wielded a pair of short swords and swung them at blurring speed. She merely closed the distance between them, ignoring the powerful blows raining down on her armor and slammed the head of her war hammer directly into the Paladin's face, causing it to burst like a dropped egg.

Now there were only a few mercenaries left on the rampart and only one ladder. Airl was closest to the ladder, but he was shooting down into the waiting throng of men on the ground. As hardly any more arrows came over the wall, Owin figured Airl had slain most of their archers.

Oriana dispatched the last mercenary on the rampart with a thrust to the throat and raised her eye patch to send the last ladder aflame. Even as fire lanced from her eye socket, Loric appeared at the top of the ladder and leapt through the stream of fire as if it were a light rain.

Oriana brought up the haft of her spear to block the wide swing from Loric's sword, but he moved even faster than the Paladins. His blade passed through her neck without slowing, and Oriana's head hit the parapet with a wet sound like rotten fruit splattering. Blood fountained from the stump of her neck as her body crumpled, the light beneath her skin snuffed out, and Owin fought a sudden urge to bring up everything he had eaten the previous day.

Even as Loric landed in a crouch next to Oriana's body, an arrow pierced his neck in a shower of blood, a mere trickle compared to the widening pool from Oriana's headless corpse. Loric paid no attention to the shaft protruding from his neck but turned aside the blow Verona aimed at his head with his sword, while sending his own mace crashing into Verona's chest, sending her toppling off the rampart and onto the waiting Azorean crowd.

Another arrow sprouted from a gap in the armor under Loric's right arm, and the Regent advanced on Airl as two more ladders swung up into place. Two Paladins appeared on top of the parapet before Ox could move toward the ladders. One leapt towards him while the other suddenly found himself engaged by Zaul, whose blurred form was much more noticeable than usual, which Owin took to mean he was getting tired.

Airl drew two long, slightly curved knives and turned aside Loric's first strike with the clear note of a struck bell before pressing his own attack.

Mercenaries poured over the parapet as three more ladders swung up. Ox removed the top portion of the Paladin's head with his double-headed ax and shoved one of the ladders off the wall. Owin reached out with his Talent to push off some of the mercenaries, but all wore unadorned leather armor. There wasn't enough metal on their person for him to push against.

Verona tried to get back up the ramp, but too many mercenaries swarmed down it, so she resolved to inflict as much damage as she could before they could reach the waiting Azoreans. Even her great strength could not hold them all back and several passed her to be met by the crowd of Azoreans, weapons already swinging. The Azorean archers no longer carried bows but stood with the rest, brandishing whatever weapons they could lay hands on.

Owin killed three more mercenaries with his flying knives, though they were a drop of water compared to the torrent of enemies still coming over the wall. He caught sight of Airl and Loric still fighting on the other side of the battlement, both attacking and dodging with inhuman speed. Airl seemed to have gotten the maul away from Loric at some point but paid a price for it as he cradled his left arm to his side and fought only with his right, a gleaming blade flashing in his fist.

Owin reached out with his Talent and pulled the sword out of Loric's grasp, letting it fall over the side of the battlement. Loric sidestepped Airl's next blow and kicked him square in the chest, sending him sprawling down onto the pitched battle on the courtyard.

Loric's fierce gaze swept across the parapet for a moment as he casually ripped out the arrow still stuck in his arm and tossed it aside. As the Regent locked eyes with Owin, he felt his heart freeze and plummet in his chest.

With a wild grimace, Loric gathered himself and leapt off into the space over the heads of the courtyard battle, tattered cape streaming behind. It must have been at least ten yards between the two sides of the battlements, but the Regent made the leap look effortless. Owin sent one of his knives straight at Loric as he soared through the air, but it rebounded off his cuirass.

As Loric landed on the top of the rampart only feet from where Owin stood, he pushed another knife at the other man's head. Loric knocked aside the knife with a quick motion of his hand, the blade snapping off of his gauntlet and spinning away before Owin could pull it back.

Owin stumbled back until he felt his back hit the stone parapet, and he grabbed for his last two daggers, but Loric was upon him before his fingers could find either hilt. The Regent seized Owin by the throat with his right hand and lifted him off the ground.

Owin found himself unable to breathe, much less pull free, as Loric had a grip of iron that easily could have snapped his neck like a flower stem. All he could do was kick his feet feebly as they hung nearly a foot off the rampart. His sight began to blur at the edges.

"You have an interesting Talent, Azorean. I've never before had such an experience; it was almost like flying. I felt closer to the Eternal than I ever have before, and I have never been surer in my purpose." Loric pulled Owin's face close to his own, ignoring Owin's fingers trying to pry his away from his throat. "Allow me to share it with you."

Loric hurled Owin away from him as easily as a child might toss a ball. Owin screamed in spite of himself and twisted about in midair as he began to fall. He looked down and saw the floor of the Colony rushing up to meet him.

Chapter Twelve

The hardest part of a battle, at least in Brigid's admittedly limited experience, was the incessant waiting. She knew it must be ten times worse for the men and women actually waiting to defend the Colony, but at least they would have the prospect of immediate mortal danger to take their minds off the tedium of waiting.

Brigid helped some of the older Azorean women, who remained behind to tend the wounded, prepare the area at the foot of the stairs, putting together crudely assembled litters and cutting up shirts and skirts for bandages. The Colony's blacksmith, a coarse, older man named Heph, worked alongside them.

She'd read a few books on roots and herbs and their use on healing, and the Colony had an impressive store of these medicinals, but she didn't think it would last the duration. Telas, who was in charge down in the Colony while Ox lead the defense, rolled out a cask of Ox's strongest spirits for the purpose of, as she put it, "washing of wounds and dulling the mind, once the willow bark poultices run out."

Brigid liked Telas and her level-headedness well enough, though she didn't much care for her choice in men. Ox seemed to be a capable leader but a bit too rough around the edges when it came to anything other than leadership; however, the frequent private conversations the pair had between them seemed to smooth out some of those edges. Brigid still found it somewhat unsettling when Telas spoke directly into her mind; it was like someone else's words rattling around in her own head.

The first wounded began to trickle down the stairway almost a half hour after the last of the Azorean defenders disappeared up the stairs. The wounded were laid out on litters and brought over to the makeshift sick bay set up around one of the Colony's wells. Their armor and weapons were stripped off as soon as they were brought down and thrown into a growing pile to be dealt with later.

The first litter Brigid reached held an older Azorean man with an arrow in his shoulder. He was not weeping or crying out in pain but rather kept up a steady commentary on how the defense was proceeding. At first, Brigid feared he was delirious but then realized he was most likely speaking to Telas, who was tending to her own litter. Brigid listened with half an ear while examining his wound.

Telas cautioned those tending to the wounded not to try to remove any arrows if there was a chance the shaft would break off, leaving the arrowhead in the wound and requiring someone to dig it out. After studying the embedded shaft for a moment, Brigid thought she'd be able to remove it in one go.

She placed the worn handle of a wooden spoon between the man's teeth and told him to brace himself. The man seemed not to have heard and kept talking around the spoon. The arrow came out after a sharp tug, and a moan of pain from the Azorean interrupted his report. She mopped up the welling blood from the wound with a wadded bandage and kept pressure on it with her elbow while she threaded a bone needle.

As she completed the first stitch, drawing the edges of the wound together, she allowed herself a moment of pride that her fingers were steady and her breathing was regular. She could remember a time when her father had badly cut his leg on a handsaw, and her mother, utterly calm, asked her to thread a needle while she held one cloth against his leg after another, each coming away shiny red as a ripe apple. Brigid had been only seven or eight at the time, and she was shaking so much she had to try nearly a dozen times to thread the needle. She remembered her mother's steely calm and tried to emulate it, refusing to acknowledge the small pit of fear growing in her middle. She knew once one gave into fear, it was very hard to bring it to heel again.

She finished sewing and poulticed the wound after pouring a measure of Ox's spirits over her handiwork. She poured another measure into a cracked tin mug and pressed it into the man's hands. She pulled the spoon from between the man's teeth and was about to move to another litter when Telas said, *"I could really use your help over here, if you please,"* into her mind, and Brigid hurried over to where the Colony Head was trying to get an Azorean with an arrow shaft sticking out of his eye to lie still. He was screaming in pain and violently shaking his head as if in denial of the wound.

"Hold his head. I need to see how far the arrow penetrated."

Brigid moved around to the man's head and grasped it as if it were a ball and forced it still. Her arms strained with effort as Telas examined the arrow and the ruins of his eye. Brigid never had seen an injured eye before and looked for a moment at the runny mess before averting her eyes. She normally had a strong stomach but figured now was not the time to measure her fortitude.

The wounded continued down the stairs, some bearing the pain in silence and others screaming in agony, and all were laid out in a row at the base of the stairs as the Azorean porters took off back up the stairs. As other female Azoreans rushed to help the fresh arrivals, Brigid offered up a silent plea to the Eternal that the trickle of wounded not become a torrent, even though she knew it was only a matter of when, not if.

Four more tended Azoreans later, Brigid began to question if her decision to stay and aid the Azoreans was the smartest decision she had ever made. Sweat beaded on her brow, and her lower back began to ache from bending over the litters.

She'd foolishly told Airl battlefield medicine would not bother her, and it hadn't, not yet, but she could feel her resolve begin to fray around the edges. The wounded were in sufficient numbers for those remaining on the canyon floor to contend with, but, from the way each Azorean around her kept glancing up at the top of the staircase, she knew they were all wondering how long they could hold out.

Brigid found her own eyes wandering over to the top of the staircase just as something flew over the edge of the canyon and began to plummet to the ground. Several Azoreans shuffling down the staircase, either with an arm around a wounded defender or carrying one with the aid of another porter, cried out in dismay, and Brigid saw the falling *something* flailing about with arms and legs.

She found herself running towards the figure even though she knew there would be nothing anyone could do after a fall from such a height. Brigid kept her eyes on the falling figure, much as she wanted to look away, and came to an abrupt stop as the person's descent began to rapidly slow for no discernible reason.

Brigid thought it was a man but couldn't see his face clearly as he continued downward at a leisurely pace, as if he weighed nothing more than a leaf falling from a bough. He had his hands pointed palm down at the ground and would have come to rest atop the pile of discarded weapons and mismatched bits of armor had he not shifted off to one side to land with a stumble and collapsed to his knees.

It was Owin, breathing in shallow gasps and thrusting his fingers through the loam of the ground as if it was the most welcome sight in the world. She almost expected him to press his face into the dirt and kiss it, as much as he liked overly showy gestures.

Brigid reached him first though Telas was just steps behind. Brigid knelt down, heedless of the dirt on her dress, and tilted Owin's chin up to look at his filthy, blood-streaked face. "Are you—what happened?" Brigid studied his face closely to see if any of the blood was his.

"Thank you, Telas. I'm not sure I would have thought to try that," Owin said, between deep breaths.

Brigid realized Telas must have been speaking to him in his mind on his way down. "Try what? How did you slow your fall?"

"Owin can move metal objects with his Talent without the need to touch them. I suspected his Talent might be used to push against stationary metal objects of sufficient size and anchorage to reverse his Talent back upon himself. Fortunately,

I was right," Telas said with a slight note of smugness that grated at Brigid.

Brigid sank back on her heels and looked at the pile of metal gear taken from the wounded Azoreans. The pile was noticeably smaller and flatter than the last time she saw it, and several of the pieces had been pushed deeply into the ground.

"No one is happier about that than me," Owin said. His breathing was coming easier. "But that took every last speck of Talent out of me. I doubt I'd be able to move as much as a thimble for a week."

"I am glad you are unharmed from the fall though the battle is going badly for us, as I'm sure you know," Telas said, glancing up at the top of the canyon. "Zaul is in almost as bad shape as Owin, and Verona and Ox together are occupying Loric for the moment, but no one is stopping the mercenaries from climbing over the wall, save Airl."

Owin rose to his feet with a groan. "What else can we do?"

"Hope those above can hold off the mercenaries long enough for some small remnant of the remaining Azoreans down here to escape," Telas said. She paused, and Brigid saw the Colony Head steel herself. "The only possible thing I can think of to try is to use the Church's own weapon against them. Airl called it the 'Crown of Glory,' I believe."

Brigid got to her feet as well and turned to the Colony Head, realization blooming like the sun. "You've been planning to use the Crown ever since Airl was stupid enough to mention it, haven't you?"

Telas eyed her coolly but made no attempt at denial. "I had no knowledge of the Crown's existence before today. I am presenting the facts, so we may make the best decision for—"

"You've already made it for him," Brigid said, trying to reign in her anger. "You're trying to browbeat him into using the Crown."

Telas frowned slightly, and her voice grew colder. "You are not his mother, and he is of age to decide for himself."

"I am standing right here," Owin interjected. "I can hear everything you're saying. The fall didn't make me deaf."

Brigid ignored him. "You don't know the risk of what you're asking; none of us do. Airl said the cost of using Blood Magic is time off your life."

"If we don't do something, we will all lose much more than that," Telas said, folding her arms. "I have heard that it is dangerous but not using it would be more so. We have no choice."

"There is always a choice!" Brigid said. "Unless you live in this Colony, it seems."

"You are a foolish village girl," Telas said quietly but with an edge that could cut iron. "Do not speak to me of choices. You've never had to make an important one in your life."

"Ladies!" Owin said, attempting to place himself between Telas and Brigid, who was gritting her teeth so hard she was surprised one didn't crack. "Let's try not to kill each other before the Church gets a chance!"

"Airl said the Crown was the most powerful talisman of Blood Magic ever made," Brigid said, grabbing Owin's arm. "It wouldn't take just minutes or hours off your life; it'll be days or weeks."

Telas visibly calmed herself. "I did not know how high the cost would be." She took Owin's other arm. "Believe me, Owin. I would use it myself if I thought I'd be able to turn the tide. Any other Azorean would do the same."

Brigid scoffed at this, but Telas continued as if she hadn't heard. "Making Ox stronger or Zaul faster won't be enough. Your Talent is different, and we'll have a chance with it."

Brigid rolled her eyes. She could tell from Owin's expression he was considering Telas' words, even though the Colony Head was manipulating him with all the subtlety of the reins and bit of a horse.

Owin was silent for several moments. He first looked at Brigid, and she merely shook her head. Nothing else she could say would change his mind one way or another, stubborn man he was. Then he looked to the wounded Azoreans coming down the stairs one at a time, their wounds no longer limited to the damage arrows could do.

Brigid never wanted to hit someone more in her life than in that moment. It seemed quite possible Telas had planned this conversation to occur in this spot, just so Owin would see the wounded Azoreans and those rushing to help. Owin's expression hardened, and Brigid knew what he would say before he opened his mouth. "Where is this Crown?"

Telas reached into the folds of her skirt and brought out from some inner pocket the box Airl had taken from Edean. "Brilliant, Telas. You missed your true purpose in life; you could have been the richest merchant in the world. You could sell a drowning man a cup of water."

"Very amusing, Miss Dorcas." Telas said frostily. "Owin failed to mention how witty a place Vridian Ford must be."

Telas opened the box but did not touch the Crown herself, Brigid noted. The Colony Head looked at it as if it were a coiled adder, but she still held the box out to Owin.

He reached out a hand to take the Crown but hesitated when Brigid said his name softly. "I know how much you owe them. This is your home now; I understand. I just want you to be able to live with this decision."

"I lost a home once, Brigid." Owin touched his chest through his ringmail as if massaging his breastbone with his fingers. He took the Crown out of the box and, just before setting it on his head, said, "I'm not going to lose another one."

Chapter Thirteen

The Crown was cold as he set it on his head. For a moment, nothing happened, and Owin was glad there wasn't a mirror handy; he didn't want to know if he looked as foolish as he felt. For a moment, he felt a mixture of relief at not having to be the person who had to somehow save the entire Colony and despair at knowing there was likely no other way to save it.

Then something within the Crown emitted a metallic *click*, and Owin felt a stab of pain as something sharp dug into his right temple, followed by another lance of pain just behind that one, and then another and another; each stab of pain followed the curving line of the Crown where the metal touched his flesh. The last was just over his left temple, and he felt the metal of the Crown warm, as if it were held over an open flame. A tingling feeling washed over his body, starting from the circle of metal on his head.

Owin felt his weariness ruthlessly pushed away, and his Talent surged into life like never before. He became aware of the location of every bit of metal around him some twenty paces in every direction, either stationary like the pendant Telas wore between her breasts, or the shattered hilt of a sword gripped in the fist of a wounded Azorean being brought down the stairs. They were all there in his mind, waiting to be noticed. If he closed his eyes, he could point right to every source of nearby metal.

"Is it working?" Telas asked, gripping the box so tightly in both hands her knuckles were white.

"It feels—" Owin searched for a word, "Freeing. As if I was only using a trickle of my Talent, and now I can use it all."

Brigid studied the Crown on his head with a frown, her arms crossed over her chest. "Don't become too confident, Owin. That Crown doesn't make you invulnerable to harm."

"Fortunately, I long ago became invulnerable to your criticism." Owin expected Brigid's frown to lessen, but it didn't. He looked up at the top of the staircase where the flow of Azoreans had ominously stopped. Porters still continued down the stairs, but no wounded appeared at the edge. Owin knew he needed to get up there as soon as possible if he had any hope of saving the Colony.

An idea occurred to him as he glanced over at the pile of weapons and gear sunk into the ground that had saved his life. Using his Talent to slow his fall was a last moment attempt, one he didn't even consider until Telas had broken into his fleeting thoughts of Vridian Ford and his family.

His idea now was the opposite of the one Telas had screamed into his mind: to use his Talent to hurl himself into the air and back up to the battle. Owin knew he never would have been able to do such a thing without the added strength of the Crown, though he tried not to think about what that was costing him. His father had once said certain situations required a man to do what he felt right and necessary and worry about the consequences later.

Owin stepped atop of the half-buried gear, and his awareness of each bit of metal intensified, so he had a clear picture in his mind of what each object looked like. He looked over at Brigid and forced a smile which she returned halfheartedly.

Telas spoke with two of the Azorean healers but kept glancing over in his direction. Owin looked back up at the top of the staircase, still devoid of any wounded Azorean, and used his Talent to seize hold of every bit of metal between his feet, nearly three dozen separate pieces. He *shoved* at the metal with his Talent. The gear sank further into the ground, but Owin kept pushing, increasing the strength he was exerting on it, and he felt the heels of his boots leave the ground. He began to rise slowly into the air, not much faster than he could climb the staircase.

He shoved harder, drawing from what felt like a vast ocean of untapped strength flowing from the Crown, sweet and eager as lust. His ascent increased in speed, and he began to hear the sounds of the battle still raging as he neared the lip of the canyon. Not wanting to continue to rise straight up, he gave one last hard push and angled his body forward so he cleared the canyon's edge. He tried his best to roll as he struck the dirt. He was on his feet much faster than normal, thanks to the grace and speed bestowed by the Crown.

The scene on the Azorean side of the battlements was utter chaos as they fought to keep the mercenaries from reaching the stairs. They held a line a few yards from the edge of the canyon, though the ground was littered with their dead or wounded. Even as Owin turned his gaze on the battle, he was bombarded with hundreds of sources of metal, too many for any one person to keep track of, but even closing his eyes did nothing to stop the overload. He had never before needed a reason to compartmentalize his Talent, but he desperately tried now and was able to shut off that particular part of his Talent after a few tense moments.

He turned back to the defense, ignoring the courtyard for the moment to see how badly the battlements were breached. Owin could see Loric atop of the parapet, guarding four ladders from Ox and Airl, who were unsuccessfully attempting to dislodge them. The ladders allowed a mercenary to climb over the wall every few moments and, while some were quickly dispatched by Airl or the Colony Head, they couldn't stop them all from joining the battle in the courtyard.

Owin seized hold of Loric's armor with his Talent, pulled him up into the air until he was suspended some ten yards over the battlements and held him in place. Ox and Airl stared up at him for a moment and, when he showed no sign of coming down, they hurried to the ladders and cast them down.

Without the Crown, it would have taken most of Owin's strength to hold Loric up in the air but required very little effort with its aid. Owin turned his attention to the mercenaries facing off against the defenders closest to him and began ripping weapons out of startled men's hands and hurling them out over the wall. A few Azoreans, upon seeing their opponents were suddenly defenseless, struck ruthlessly and several weaponless mercenaries and members of the Church died where they stood while the rest of the Azoreans contented themselves with stepping back to take a breath and keep a wary eye on the disarmed mercenaries.

Owin was able to disarm two or three at a time, and he pushed his way into the throng of bodies, heading for the ramp and disarming as he went. Some of the mercenaries tried to gang up on individual Azoreans and take their weapons, but this quickly stopped when most who tried were killed without hesitation. Some of the others Owin disarmed ran for the ramp, thinking to escape over the ladders; instead Ox or Airl swiftly dispatched them.

Owin reached the base of the ramp, having disarmed dozens of the enemy soldiers, all while keeping Loric aloft. As he climbed the ramp, he saw Loric finish unbuckling his cuirass and fall from between the front and back plates to land perfectly balanced upon the parapet's edge. Owin cast the empty armor over the wall, even as Loric threw aside his sword, gauntlets and all other visible metal, save for the gold bracelets encircling each wrist.

Even without the Crown, Owin would have known the Regent still had metal on his person, though hidden beneath a white shirt that lay plastered with sweat to his chest. With his enhanced Talent, he picked out two sources of metal under his shirt, each piercing his chest just over his rib cage, and Owin could tell they were elaborately carved metal spikes with large heads that sat flush with Loric's skin.

Loric smiled as Owin reached the top of the ramp, his eyes aflame with mocking hatred. "You are quite resilient, Azorean." He took a step toward Owin, casually, as if he had all the time he wished. "Know you die with honor. I can't remember the last Azorean I killed with my bare hands." Loric lunged with blinding speed, hands outstretched to wrap around Owin's throat.

Without the aid of the Crown, he never would have had time to dodge, but with the inhuman speed of the Blessing, he sidestepped Loric's lunge easily. The Regent recovered quickly and stared at Owin. His eyes flicked upward to the Crown resting on Owin's head, and they widened in disbelief.

"The Crown of Glory?" Loric's voice was barely a whisper. "To think of it tainted by the foul blood of an Azorean . . . if I could wear it—"

While Loric was speaking, Owin seized hold of both metal spikes piercing the Regent's chest and pulled sharply. Instead of being pulled from his body, Loric stumbled forward as if shoved from behind. "Your filthy Azorean tricks are no match for the Eternal's Blessing," Loric sneered, recovering his footing.

Before he could make another move, Owin seized hold of the gold bracelets encircling the Regent's wrists and pulled his arms out to each side, holding him in place. Owin was using only a trickle of the torrent of strength waiting to be tapped, and he knew ripping both arms from Loric's body required only a mere thread more of strength. He didn't think he could bring himself to actually do it. He increased the pull on both of Loric's arms until he heard a sharp crack as one of the Regent's shoulders dislocated. Loric gave a grunt of pain but kept his face impassive.

"Tell your men to sound a retreat," Owin said, trying not to let his voice quaver, "or I will rip both of your arms off."

Loric gritted his teeth and glared at Owin. "Do your worse, filth. The Eternal will see me avenged."

The Regent's gaze shifted to Owin's side, and Owin became aware of Ox standing next to him, his armor sporting several large cracks and dents, and a large slash down one side of his face slowly staining a hastily wrapped bandage red. The Colony Head hefted his double-headed ax in his right hand and swung it one handed at Loric's restrained body, shearing his head off at the neck.

The head hit the rampart and rolled off into the courtyard trailing gore as it went. Owin lifted the corpse until it was clear of the parapet and hurled it away. The body easily crested the mound of trees in the distance and disappeared.

"It was the only way," Ox muttered, unable to open his mouth because of the bandage. Owin nodded, glad he didn't have to be the one to do it. As it was, he felt the unsettling feeling at the back of his throat that always preceded his throwing up but was able to keep everything down.

A horn sounded over the field of battle, a single note long and deep, and the mercenaries and members of the Church still on the field turned and headed back for the copse of trees, leaving their dead or wounded companions where they lay. Small shapes lazily circled high in the sky over the field of battle, and Owin knew they must be vultures and other carrion eaters, eyeing the feast spread out before them.

Owin turned and looked down at the courtyard where the fighting had ended not long after he had disarmed most of the mercenaries. Perhaps a dozen Azoreans with spears watched over easily twice their number of mercenaries, all of whom stood packed tightly together, sullen and angry.

Other than the Azorean guards, only four others remained standing in the courtyard, and they were busy shifting dead Azoreans onto litters one at a time before bringing them down the stairs. Owin saw ten bodies remaining, though he didn't know how many had already disappeared down the stairs.

The opening through which he and Ox passed through to get to the battlefield appeared again with loud grinding of stone against stone. Owin saw Roland appear at the top of the stairs. He expected at least one of the prisoners to try to escape through the newly formed opening, but none took a step toward it, though more than one looked at it with longing.

Several Azoreans came up the staircase after Roland, each one carrying a large wicker pannier on their back and headed out onto the field of battle, most likely to collect spoils. They all wore long knives or short hatchets at their belts. Telas and Verona appeared after the last pannier carrier, and Owin followed the other Colony Head down the ramp.

Telas smiled broadly at the pair of them, her hair piled atop her head in a tight bun, as they stepped off the ramp and swept Owin into a tight hug, much to his surprise, murmuring thanks into his ear. When she released him to embrace Ox, the big Azorean muttered his thanks as well, somewhat resentfully, as if he expected to be the first to be embraced by his lover.

Verona glanced at them once and, after seeing they were both in one piece, planted herself in front of the captured mercenaries so each man could see her, fists on her hips. She no longer wore her battered armor, but one of her low cut dresses. Blood smeared her left shoulder and trickled from a thin gash, and the hair on the side of her head was matted with more blood, though both wounds might as well have not existed for all the attention she paid them. Her teeth were stained red and she looked quite ferocious as she bared them in a fierce smile.

"Listen up you pissant mercenary scum! You will be held here until midday tomorrow and then you will be free to leave. If any of you are having thoughts of climbing down those stairs to ask for help, I will personally knock out each tooth left to you one at a time."

For the first time, Owin got a good look at the mercenary's feet and saw each man had their boots encased in solid rock, up to their knees. The rock was smooth and looked to have been wrapped about boots and shins for centuries. Owin marveled at Roland's handiwork and glanced back at the Azorean who was leaning against the rock wall and reading from a thick book, totally oblivious to his surroundings.

The mercenary closest to Verona turned his head and spat on the ground. He stood two heads taller than her and twice as broad with a puckered scar running down the side of his face and disappearing beneath his ring mail.

"That's an awful big mouth on you, Azorean. Let's see if it's big enough." He leered down at Verona, and several mercenaries smirked. Verona said nothing in response but grabbed his right arm in both hands and broke his beefy forearm as effortlessly as another woman might snap a fresh carrot. The mercenary gave a howl of pain and cradled his arm, now featuring an extra joint, against his chest. The smirks vanished. One of the prisoners at the front closed his eyes and began muttering a prayer under his breath.

"If anyone else wants to say something, by all means speak up. I quite enjoy the sound a bone makes when it snaps," Verona announced, the closest thing to pleasantness Owin ever heard in her voice.

All the men were quiet, save for the whimpers of pain coming from the wounded mercenary. Verona waited expectantly, shifting her gaze over the motionless men and waiting for one to meet it. One of the mercenaries toward the back of the group finally asked, "What about food?"

"Why do you think we've allowed you to keep your leathers? I've heard it's very tough to chew, but I'm sure you won't mind as much tomorrow." Verona turned and headed out through the open hole in the battlements.

Owin looked across the slowly emptying courtyard to where Airl sat cross-legged on the ground near the last remaining bundle of arrows. His right arm was in a sling, and he was trying unsuccessfully to untie the grubby string holding the bundle together with one hand, cursing under his breath. Owin drew his last remaining dagger at his belt and, crouching next to Airl, cut open the bundle. "Thanks. Both of my knives are out there somewhere, buried in the heads of two different Paladins." Airl said casually, as if commenting on the weather.

Airl glanced up at the Crown resting on Owin's head and then back down as he picked up the first arrow from the bundle, sighting down the shaft before setting it aside. "So, you're the one they convinced to put that on." Airl said it nonchalantly, and Owin was unsure how to respond, so he merely said, "Yes."

Airl picked up and discarded a few more arrows before he asked, "Did they tell you the price Blood Magic will take from you?"

"Brigid said it would shorten my life," Owin replied. He hesitated, wavering between knowledge and ignorance. Airl continued sorting through arrows and finally found one he deemed suitable enough to slip into his empty quiver after discarding over a dozen. Owin decided he would rather know the answer than to spend the rest of his life wondering, so he asked, "Do you know how much time I've lost?"

"It'd be hard to tell, especially with how strong the Crown of Glory is supposed to be. What did you do with it?"

Owin described the huge jump from the canyon floor and the other things he had done with his Talent since putting on the Crown. Airl absently turned an arrow end over end between his long fingers while he considered, and said, "I'm not expert on the subject by any means, but I'd wager you spent no less than six months of your life to save the Colony."

Owin nodded slowly. He was a little relieved having thought the cost would be much higher. "Can I take the Crown off now?"

"Most Blessings cannot be taken off, save in death, but I'd be surprised if the Crown of Glory had the same limitation." Airl continued sorting through the bundle of arrows, still with only one in his quiver.

Owin reached up to touch the Crown, the metal warm beneath his fingers but hesitated as Airl said, "Not yet. When you remove the Blessing you will most likely faint from the fatigue the Crown has suppressed." Airl met Owin's gaze, his expression unreadable. "The Crown is linked to you now until you die. No one else will be able to do anything with it. If I were you, I'd drop it into that pit by the secret passage and forget about it. If the Church ever learns you have it, they will stop at nothing to kill you to reclaim it."

"I don't think they know I have it. Loric seemed to be the only one to recognize it, and he's not going to be reporting anything." Owin said, trying to sound hopeful.

"This is not something that should be left to chance. You need to assume the Church knows the Colony has their most powerful Blessing, and . . ." Airl paused, considering his statement for a moment before abruptly changing the subject. "My pardon, but something just occurred to me I have to see to."

He stood up suddenly, setting aside his quiver. He touched Owin's shoulder for a moment. "Thank you for what you did. I was beginning to think today would be the end of my long journey, and I'm not ready for it to finish just yet." Airl headed for the hole in the battlement leading out to the field and disappeared through it.

Chapter Fourteen

Night was falling when Telas summoned Owin to a meeting in the library. Most of the unwounded Azoreans had retired early after laboring for several hours, cleaning up and tending to the wounded, and digging far too many graves at the far end of the Colony.

Since the Unbroken Church had fully retreated from the field of battle, Owin had been busy. Using the limitless strength of the Crown, he'd been able to use his Talent to float the rest of the Azorean dead down to the floor of the canyon, in groups of three and four, taking the utmost care to set them down gently at the base of the staircase. He then used his enhanced strength and speed to help out with the clean up effort where he could, steadily drawing upon the Crown to keep himself refreshed and his growing exhaustion at bay.

When he received the summons, he sped over to his hut to change out of his dirty, blood-stained armor, pulled on a clean shirt and headed for the library. Those who Owin passed on his way to the meeting all paused to shake his hand or clap him on the back, offering up words of thanks. One Azorean woman, only a few years older than himself, hugged him to her not inconsiderable bosom and whispered in his ear she had a more tangible means of thanks she wanted to impart on him, but he'd have to stop at her mound later to collect.

Owin felt embarrassed at all the praise, especially the whispered offer he'd have to give serious thought to, and a part of him felt as if he should share exactly what that day's victory had cost him, though he kept it to himself.

The steady ring of hammer on anvil came from Heph's tent, and Owin considered stopping in for just a moment, then remembered the Colony Heads were waiting for him. Firelight came from the windows of the Mess which remained open much later than normal.

Owin entered the study to find Airl, Brigid, Verona, Telas and Ox already seated at the table. Bone-deep weariness lay etched in each face as they turned to look at him. Ox's face was still partially covered with a clean bandage, and Owin could see a bright red line slashing down the side of his right arm, gleaming with white stitches. Of the three women present, Verona was the only one who bore physical wounds. Her left shoulder was bound in bandages, and Owin could see her hair was partially shaved so stitches could close the wound on the side of her head. Airl no longer had his arm in a sling and seemed to bear no other injury.

Owin took one of the two remaining empty chairs next to Brigid, who smiled in greeting but said nothing. He stared for a moment at the last empty chair, a bloodied, empty eye patch resting on the table, its owner's absence noticeable as a missing tooth in a wide grin. Owin had respected Oriana, certainly, and the Mistress of Arms was more friendly than Verona or Zaul, but he still felt as though he had barely known her, despite all the hours spent training with her. He missed her presence more than Zaul's, who was laid up in the large area set aside for the more grievously wounded, though the self- proclaimed 'Fastest Azorean Alive' only suffered from a broken leg and some shallow slashes across his chest and was already boasting of the three Paladins and dozens of mercenaries he had killed in the battle.

"Now that the Colony's Hero is here, can we get on with this?" Verona asked, turning back to Telas.

The Colony Head frowned at Verona but addressed the room as a whole. "I know we're all tired, especially those of us who did the actual fighting, but there is a small matter we need to discuss before we turn in." Telas looked at each person seated around the table, her eyes lingering on Oriana's empty chair. "While out foraging for spoils among the enemy dead, three dead Paladins were found and stripped of their Blessings. The pieces were given to Ox, and he has secured them."

Verona leaned forward slightly in her chair as if Ox might produce them at any moment, and she wanted to be the first to lay claim to one. Telas waited for her to say something, but, when she remained silent, the Colony Head continued. "Ox and I have yet to decide to do with them. However, Ox tells me he and Airl slew at least four Paladins between them, which means at least one of the Azoreans sent out to scavenge kept at least one piece for themselves."

"If you tell me who went out to scavenge, I'm sure I could persuade the guilty Azorean to reconsider," Verona said.

"That won't be necessary," Telas replied. "Ox and I are of the opinion those Azoreans responsible merely thought the implements were regular spoils of the battle."

Verona leaned back in her chair, crossing her arms under her breasts. "If you've already decided this, then why are we bloody sitting here?"

"Because," Airl said quietly, "Telas wants you all here when she accuses me of taking the missing Blessing." All eyes turned to the archer, who smiled mirthlessly and held up his arms in mock surrender. "I freely confess to taking it, and three others off the slain Paladins. They need to be destroyed."

Verona scowled at Airl, and Ox said, "That is your opinion, Airl."

"Yes, it is, just as those Blessings are mine. They were free for the taking, under the Articles of War signed by the ruling parties of both Realms over three hundred years ago. They are mine to do with as I wish, and I choose not to let the

Colony have them." Airl was the perfect vision of calm, his voice level as a still pond.

"I've seen you fight, Airl. Why do you want them? The Colony needs them much more than you do." Ox said, glancing at Telas as Verona openly glared at Airl.

"The Colony needs them as much as they need an arrow to the forehead." Airl said. "You've dealt the Unbroken Church a hard blow today, one they will not recover from quickly. If Azoreans start using the Church's own weapons openly, they will return twice as strong to reclaim them, doubtless with help from one or both Realms. No one will be content to let you keep such powerful weapons."

"If they are so desperate to have these things back," Telas said, "where will they look first when their scouts don't find them among the dead tonight? If the Colony has them, we stand a much greater chance of defeating them again."

"They will suspect their own mercenaries first, especially those you've taken prisoner. They will put each one to the question, but, even with the resources of the Church, it will take some time, as I'm sure all the mercenaries scattered to the wind as soon as they were paid after the battle."

"I'm not sure that is a chance the Colony can take," Ox said. "What'll you take for the Blessings you have?"

"There's nothing you could offer I'd trade them for." Airl answered. "I'm only holding on to them myself until I can put them beyond all reach. I'd shatter or melt them down tonight if it were possible."

Verona started to say something with her fist raised to pound on the surface of the table when Telas stared at her coldly, and Owin figured she must have spoken privately in her mind, for she closed her mouth and didn't say anything. She did bring her fist down onto the surface of the table, sending out fine cracks radiating in all directions from the point of impact.

Airl ignored her silent outburst and leaned his elbows against the table as he looked steadily at Telas. "While we're on the subject of interrogation, how did Owin acquire such a dashing head accessory? I feel quite sure it was secured in its box when I left it with my things I foolishly assumed would not be riffled through."

Ox frowned across the table at Airl. "Come now, that's not—" The big Azorean broke off as Telas touched his arm and then met Airl's gaze. "We were losing, Airl. You know that; had I not acted, we would not be sitting here now."

"That's probably true," Airl said, "though it doesn't explain how you were able to open the box so quickly when it took me several hours to work it out. The Hero of the Colony here," Airl indicated Owin with his chin, "was gone from the battle for less than a quarter of an hour."

Ox leveled a thick forefinger across the table at Airl. "What are you accusing her of? Telas would not enter your mind without asking."

"I did." Telas said quietly, and all eyes in the room turned to her. Ox looked as if someone had hit him full in the face with a sack of rocks. "I didn't mean for it to happen, but I cannot deny it did. When you told us about the box earlier, the secret to opening it appeared on the very surface of your mind, so unavoidable for me to notice it may as well have been tattooed on your forehead." Ox placed a large hand gently on her shoulder, and she placed her much smaller one atop his. "It happens, sometimes, if a person is concentrating hard on a task or powerful emotion."

"I see," Airl said, his voice as flat as the stone table before him. "Regardless, I have too much else in my mind that doesn't need to be known by anyone else." He straightened and walked over to where his bow and quiver lay propped against the wall.

Verona turned to Ox. "Are we just going to let him leave with those? He was handy to have around in a battle but think of how many Azoreans we lost. We need every Blessing we can get hold of." Ox didn't answer but kept his gaze on Telas, who stared down at the blank expanse of the table, her face impassive.

Airl pulled his mostly empty quiver over his head and hefted his still strung bow. "You are welcome to try to stop me, Verona, though even your strength won't be much help when you're stuck full of arrows." Without waiting for a response, he looked over at Brigid, his voice softening. "Miss Dorcas, if I might have a word or three?"

Owin tried to meet her eye as she got up, but she kept her gaze on Airl, the beginnings of a smile on her lips. Owin wondered if perhaps the older man had been more than a guide and guard on the journey from Barwick but then reminded himself who the particular girl in question was. Still, Brigid was a woman beneath everything else, and Owin had not heard of her being involved with anyone in Vridian Ford or nearby, so she had to start somewhere.

The pair stood close together and spoke in low enough voices that Owin could not pick out anything they were saying. He turned back around and saw Ox still staring at Telas, his lips moving slightly, and he knew they were in one of their private conversations. Verona stared at Owin, or rather, the Crown of Glory, apparently lost in thought.

After a few moments of silence, Owin glanced back at the pair and saw Airl shake hands with Brigid, smiling fondly down at her, as a father might to his favorite daughter. Then he turned and left the study without another word or glance back.

Brigid stood where she was, her arms folded and her head slightly bowed as if examining her boots. If it had been any other woman, Owin would have thought she were pulling herself together so as not to cry, but he'd never met a woman *less* likely to cry than Brigid.

Verona pushed her chair back and rose to her feet. She glanced at the Colony Heads and frowned slightly before she walked out of the room, not sparing a glance for either Owin or Brigid. Owin waited a few moments more and walked over to where Brigid still stood and said, "You look like he just told you he was the Eternal incarnate."

Brigid visibly shook herself, as if coming out of a daydream, though her expression of astonishment remained. "Not far off." She met his eyes and grinned wistfully. "He's Airl. *The* Airl." Brigid placed dcfinite emphasis on the word as if it would remove all doubt. She watched his reaction expectantly, as if the name would bring about the same look of wonder to Owin's face, but he looked at her, nonplussed. "So? His first name is The?"

Now Brigid's expression changed to one of incredulity, an expression much more at home on her face. "You can't be serious. Airl, of the Nine? *The Heroes of a Hundred Tales*?"

Owin frowned slightly, recalling the book title. "I thought that was all made up."

"You fought beside one of the Nine Heroes! Finally you can say you've done something worthwhile in your life!"

Owin ignored the barb, still unconvinced. "He'd have to be centuries old. That Airl fellow was old but not a dried out skeleton!"

"You saw how good he was with that bow," Brigid said, ticking off points on her fingers. "He healed very fast; I can attest to that. He made at least one reference to Ghent, another member of the Nine."

Owin paused for a moment, thinking back to when he'd spoken with the archer right after the battle, when Airl's arm had been in a sling. "Could be some—"

"Azoreans are not the monsters we've been taught since birth to hate and avoid. If that's true, how much more ridiculous is the idea that Airl is one of the Nine?"

Owin opened his mouth to retort but found he had nothing to say. Instead, he grinned at Brigid. "Are you admitting all the world's answers aren't in books?"

Brigid threw up her hands. "*Anyway*, I've decided to stay here at the Colony for a bit. I need to stay and collect information for my book."

Now it was Owin's turn to look incredulously at her. "*Stay* at the Colony? What about your parents?"

Brigid waved a hand as if this was of no importance. "I'll send a raven; they'll understand."

"When did you decide to write a book?"

Brigid gave him a flat look as if he were being deliberately thick. "I decided hours ago, Owin; try to keep up. I'm going to write my book on Azoreans. There's hardly anything written about them, and I expect people might buy it just to see if all their fear and hatred are justified. Then I'm going to go to the House of Commons in the Northern Realm and not let those old men sleep a moment until they read my book and agree to start a discussion about changing some laws about Azoreans." Brigid grinned, her eyes twinkling, as if she couldn't wait to get started.

Owin couldn't help but grin as well, though as he did, he felt the Crown shift slightly as his scalp pulled on the hollow needles imbedded under his skin. Brigid kept talking excitedly about her book, but Owin found himself listening with only half an ear.

Even after he took off the Crown, he knew he would be far from free of it, just as he knew he would spend quiet moments in the upcoming days thinking about the months of his life he had traded for the salvation of the Colony. Owin knew, deep down, the trade was worth it, even if it had cost ten times as much. Certainly, his father, a mayor who always tried to do right for the whole of Vridian Ford, could understand.

Owin had to smile to himself at that; putting on the Crown had shown more responsibility than anything he could have done at Vridian Ford, though his father might never know it. A gentle blow to his forehead brought him back out of his thoughts.

"Did I say something funny, Owin Cadmon?" Brigid asked, pulling her hand back and folding her arms, "or were you just daydreaming like you always did in school?"

"Not at all, Miss Dorcas. Please continue."

Epilogue

Icilius Kelelm stood before the closed doors leading to the High Regent's private office and looked at the engravings tracing the edges of the doors, not really seeing them. He always thought his first time setting foot inside the High Regent's office would be one of great personal significance and reverence; there were few places more holy in the entire Citadel, as it was said the High Regent sometimes communed directly with Elanmil, the Eternal's personal avatar through whom He passed His most important commands, for no human, no matter how pious, could withstand the sound of the Eternal's True Voice.

Instead of feeling elated, all Icilius could feel was a weariness that clung to his bones like lead weights. He'd only slept a few of the last seventy two hours since the disastrous battle against the Middle Realm, seeing to a hundred different tasks which fell to him, now Regent Loric was dead and he, Icilius, was now the ranking Paladin.

He shuddered even now as he remembered, watching with his own eyes enhanced by his Blessing from the command tent erected in a copse of trees, as Regent Loric's head was hacked from his body with no more care than one took at a slaughterhouse. Icilius seized the horn from the closest trumpeter he could find, breaking two of the man's fingers in his haste and blew a single sorrowful note of retreat.

Icilius had made sure the remnants of his forces began the long trek back to the Citadel before he began to run on ahead to make his report in person and take responsibility for the colossal failure, even though it hadn't been his command. Upon reaching the Citadel, he ignored all inquiries and solicitations for information and made his way to see the High Regent, not even stopping to change into clean leathers. His were mud-stained and reeked of sweat and blood.

Icilius raised a fist and rapped twice on the door.

"Come!"

Icilius pushed open the right hand door and crossed the threshold onto a thick, lush blue carpet that felt odd under his worn boots after running so many miles on packed dirt and cobblestones.

The High Regent sat in a high-backed chair behind his large, crescent-shaped desk. His face was impassive, and he watched Icilius close the door and cross the office to stand in front of his desk before he said anything.

Icilius snapped a perfect salute and considered prostrating himself on the ground before the High Regent but did not trust himself to not fall asleep in the middle of giving his report, extra strength given by the Blessing or no. He saw several slips of paper lying on the desk before the High Regent and knew them to be missives sent during and after the battle via raven.

The High Regent did not look up at Icilius to acknowledge the salute but stared down at the missives on his desk, drumming one thick forefinger on the desk in a steady staccato beat. Icilius waited, still holding the salute and feeling sweat tickle its way down his spine. He could think of nothing he wanted more than to sleep, although a wash and a clean uniform was a close second.

The High Regent spoke quietly as if musing to himself. "You are the ranking Paladin remaining alive from the pilgrimage. Nine of the Citadel's finest fighting men dead at the hands of the vilest scum in all of Irillia; yet you, one barely a month from First Blood, still live? Report."

Icilius dropped the salute even though he had not received permission. He remained standing rigidly still, his arms at his sides. He told of the battle and defeat as concisely as he could, how he had been commanded by Regent Loric to remain out of the battle and observe and every command he had given after he sounded the retreat. Before he reached the part in his retelling where he took off for the Citadel, the High Regent held up a hand, and Icilius shut his mouth with a sharp click of teeth.

"You followed standard battle protocol and retrieved the fallen Paladin's Blessings, did you not?"

This was one of the points of the conversation Icilius had been dreading. It was the type of sensitive information he dared not have included in his missives to the Citadel, and so it fell to him to break the news in person. "Yes, High Regent. Not all could be found, however."

The High Regent brought his palm down on the top of his polished desk with a sharp crack. "Did they vanish into thin air? Surely you thought to check those mercenary thugs before you paid them?"

"Yes, High Regent. They were all searched thoroughly for stolen spoils before allowed to leave."

"What about the Clerics?"

"High Regent, I do not think any of the Clerics under my command would knowingly withhold Blessings for their own gain. They are all Eternal-fearing men, and would—" Icilius cut himself off as the High Regent rose to his feet and circled his desk, moving with far more grace and speed than his advanced years should allow. Now that Icilius was more familiar with how the Blessings worked, he knew the High Regent must be using one, though Icilius could not see it on his person.

The High Regent stopped directly before Icilius, who had to restrain himself from throwing himself down in obeisance.

Even though the High Regent stood a hand shorter than himself, Icilius felt as if the older man was towering over him. "I pride myself in being a man of some intellect, Paladin." The High Regent said in a low voice couched in anger. "It would seem you are suggesting the Azorean wretches have their diseased hands on property of the Unbroken Church."

Icilius nodded, not trusting his voice to remain steady. As he was continually drawing on his Blessing to remain upright, he was able to see the High Regent's blow before it landed and forced himself not to move out of the way.

The High Regent's backhanded slap slammed against his face, and Icilius rolled with the blow, throwing himself to the side and landing hard on his knees. He waited for another blow to fall, staring at the High Regent's gilt-edged slippers, but another was not forthcoming. "Aside from gross incompetence, why are you here in the Citadel and not taking back those Blessings?"

"High Regent, I thought only if I were to attempt to retrieve the stolen property on my own without even a single other Paladin for backup, the only possible outcome would be the Azoreans possessing yet another Blessing."

"Bah!" The High Regent spat, and he turned and strode back toward his desk, hands clasped behind his back. Instead of sitting back down at his desk, he stood before the large windows set into the wall behind his desk, pristine lengths of *Aian* glass looking down onto the expanse of the Anidor Ocean hundreds of feet below. The High Regent muttered something under his breath, and Icilius had to concentrate *not* to hear it, even without the enhancement his Blessing bestowed upon his senses.

"If you've finished your report, Paladin, you may leave." The High Regent did not turn back around. "There is much to consider before I can correct this monumental failure."

As much as Icilius would have liked to leave for food and his bed, he said, "There is another matter I need to speak to you about, High Regent. Questionable tactics used by Regent Loric under the flag of parley."

Icilius waited for a response from the older man, but, when he remained silent, Icilius continued, explaining how Loric took several children from Barwick's orphan asylum under questionable pretenses and how they'd been forced to take part in his plan to ambush the Azorean parley party.

"Of greater interest to me, Paladin, is how you so callously malign the man's name while his corpse is still cooling. This is in very poor taste."

"I can assure you, I had— have nothing but respect for him. I only thought such an act went against some of the Eternal's teachings."

"Enough!" The High Regent's voice boomed, sudden and terrible like thunder from a clear sky. He turned from the windows, eyes narrowed and lips razor thin. "You forget your place, Paladin! You are nothing but a tool for our great Church to use as I see fit! Does a carpenter seek advice from his hammer?"

The High Regent had taken a few steps toward Icilius but then seemed to think better of it and sat down behind his desk, staring at Icilius over steepled fingers, remarkably wrinkle-free despite his advanced age. "The Eternal has charged me with ridding the world of that Azorean rabble, and it shall be done by any means necessary. Any sins the Church is forced to commit in the name of accomplishing this goal will be lain at the feet of the Azorean worms, for they have caused our sin by their very existence." His voice no longer boomed, though his eyes were alight with a fervor that froze Icilius' marrow with dread.

Icilius bowed deeply, asked for the High Regent's forgiveness and left the lavishly decorated room. As the door closed behind him, he felt a quiet resolve suffuse his entire being, not unlike the strength given by his Blessing. There was something wrong with the High Regent; a black canker that threatened to consume the Church entirely. A sin was a sin;

there was no excuse for it, and blame could not be conveniently passed to someone else.

Icilius refused to believe the Eternal would agree with the High Regent's proclamation of deferred sin, and the inescapable truth bloomed in his mind even as he walked down the hallway; the High Regent had fallen from the Eternal's favor and was steering the Church as he wished.

This could not stand, and Icilius was the only one who could do something about it.

Acknowledgments

I'd like to thank Eureka College and its far-too-early Monday morning Creative Writing Classes for first draft critiques, as well as Joel Shoemaker and Lisa Kelly for their support in reading later drafts. Thank you also to R.T. Lovatto, Timmy Bauer and Eric Sweetman, whose tremendous artistic talent created the cover and map illustrations. Thank you Mom and Dad, for your love and support, and for instilling in me a great love of reading at an early age.

Mostly, I'd like to thank my wonderful wife Cassie, who provided tireless support and endless edits. She helped me realize my dream of being a published author, and I only hope I can help her realize her own dreams half as well as she's aided me in realizing mine.

About the Author

Patrick Williams lives in Central Florida with his beautiful wife and works in the hospitality industry. *Chasm of Talent* is his first published book, but far from the first written. He's currently working on a trilogy of books taking place in Irillia, set some fifty years after the events of *Chasm*.

www.ingramcontent.com/pod-product-compliance
Lightning Source LLC
Chambersburg PA
CBHW060357180626
46817CB00007B/2455